NEVER TRUST A
DEAD MAN

Also by Vivian Vande Velde

Smart Dog

Ghost of a Hanged Man

A Coming Evil

Curses, Inc. and Other Stories

Tales from the Brothers Grimm and the Sisters Weird

Companions of the Night

Dragon's Bait

User Unfriendly

A Well-Timed Enchantment

A Hidden Magic

Vivian Vande Velde

NEVER TRUST A
DEAD MAN

Harcourt Brace & Company
San Diego   New York   London

Requests for permission to make copies of any part of the work should
be mailed to: Permissions Department, Harcourt Brace & Company,
6277 Sea Harbor Drive, Orlando, Florida 32887-6777.

Library of Congress Cataloging-in-Publication Data
Vande Velde, Vivian.
Never trust a dead man/Vivian Vande Velde.
p.   cm.
Summary: Wrongly convicted of murder and punished by being sealed
in the tomb with the dead man, seventeen-year-old Selwyn enlists the
help of a witch and the resurrected victim to find the true killer.
ISBN 0-15-201899-9
[1. Murder—Fiction.   2. Mystery and detective stories.]
I. Title.
PZ7.V285117Ne   1999
[Fic]—dc21   98-39885

Text set in Janson MT
Designed by Lori McThomas Buley

C E F D
Printed in the United States of America

To Gloria and Terry,
whose sense of humor—
as scary as that might seem—
matches mine

NEVER TRUST A
DEAD MAN

ONE

✛

For Selwyn Roweson, the morning the villagers turned on him started the way the night before had ended: He and his father were removing tree stumps from the bit of land they hoped to plant as an additional field next spring. "Because even if you won't be marrying Anora after all," his father had said, "you'll be getting married sometime, and you'll be needing the extra land."

Selwyn was inclined to think his father hoped that pulling and hacking at stubborn tree stumps would be enough to drive Anora from Selwyn's mind—which just went to show how simple parents could be about certain matters.

"Besides," his father told him, "a wispy little town

girl isn't right for farm life. What you need to find yourself is a big, sturdy woman."

"Big?" repeated Selwyn, barely able to spare the breath as he wielded the ax at one of the tree roots, sending wood chips flying onto his clothes and into his hair. "Sturdy?" He himself was of a small build—and, at seventeen years old, not likely to gain much more height or breadth. The last thing he wanted was a wife bigger and stronger than he was. "Are we talking about a wife or a pair of oxen?"

"Well," his father said, as though giving the matter due consideration, "of course, that would be *your* choice. Oxen are very good at removing tree stumps. On the other hand, their after-dinner conversation is generally mediocre at best, and they can hardly dance at all. Maybe, instead, you could find a girl who's big and sturdy, but not *too* big and sturdy."

Selwyn laughed, though mostly with relief that the ax blade had finally split the root.

He put down the ax and picked up the shovel.

The day was unseasonably warm, being that time of year when the autumn leaves have fallen but the winter snow has not, and Selwyn's shirt stuck wetly to his back. He paused, straightening, for a moment's rest and to blow his hair out of his eyes.

That was when he saw the villagers approaching.

"Father," he said, never for a moment mistaking their intention to be to help dig up tree stumps, for several carried staffs or clubs, and all looked grim.

The last of the smile faded from his father's face, but

his voice was jovial as he called out to the dozen or fifteen men approaching. "What is it? What's wrong? Tell me we're not at war again."

It was a reasonable query, for—of all of them—only Selwyn's father had gone away to be in the king's army, which was how he came so late to marrying that he was almost fifty years old with a son of seventeen. The villagers had turned to him before for help with soldiers that had crossed the border, or with bandits raiding on the road to Saint Hilda's, or—once—with two feuding wizards who nearly leveled Orik's tavern trying to settle their differences.

But his father didn't think this was the case; Selwyn could tell the lightness in his voice was forced.

And any lingering doubts were ended when Thorne, who was in the lead, called back, "Put down the shovel, Rowe."

Which was such an odd thing to say no matter why they were here that Selwyn felt a flutter of dread in the pit of his stomach even though Thorne was their neighbor and had farmed the land nearest theirs for longer than Selwyn had been alive.

His father, who before that had had no reason to hold on to his shovel, looked at Thorne and the oncoming crowd appraisingly. He jammed the shovel into the pile of dirt he and Selwyn had dug up from around the latest stump's roots, and rested his arm on top of the handle, where it was still in ready reach.

The villagers stopped, five or six paces away. A shovel's length away.

"Step over here, boy," said Linton, the miller's nephew, though Selwyn didn't yet know the significance of that.

"Stay," Selwyn's father ordered, as though Selwyn had no sense at all.

"We just want to talk to him," Thorne said.

"Fine. Talk," Selwyn's father said. "His hearing's good."

Thorne met his stare for several long moments. Then he said, "Farold's dead. Murdered last night in the mill."

Farold was another of Derian Miller's nephews, Linton's cousin. Selwyn was shocked that someone had been murdered in their quiet community, but not dismayed that it was Farold. Relieved, in fact, that it was Farold and no one else. Pleased, if truth be told, that if it had to happen to someone, it had happened to Farold. But he knew not to let any such thing show on his face. He tried to think nice thoughts only. Farold wasn't all that bad, exactly, he told himself. Farold was better than...Well, he was better than sitting down on a tack. He was better than breaking a tooth on a peach pit.

His father asked, "What makes you think Selwyn did it?"

So much for nice thoughts. Though, in truth, it was the only reason they could be here, looking the way they looked. How could they think he'd kill someone—even obnoxious, swaggering Farold? But Thorne was staring right at him, finally addressing *him* and not his father, asking him, "*Did* you?"

It took several tries to get his voice to work. "No," he said, amazed that Thorne—who had known him all his life—could even ask with a straight face.

"Well then," Thorne said reasonably.

That couldn't possibly be it, Selwyn knew. They couldn't have marched all this way from Penryth just to turn around and walk back at a single-word declaration of innocence.

"We were all here," Selwyn's father told them. "Last night, you say? We were right here, all four of us, all night—me, the boy, his mother, and his grandmother. We'll all vouch for him."

That caused a shiver down his back, which Selwyn tried to disguise as brushing away a fly. He crossed his arms over his chest defiantly.

"Fine," Thorne said. "Come back to the village, explain everything to Bowden. See if there's anything you know that can possibly help us determine who *did* kill him."

The faces beyond Thorne didn't look quite so convinced, so reasonable.

"I've just explained to you," his father said. "And as for the rest: Any number of people would be glad to have Farold dead." He looked right at Linton then, which could have been by way of apology for speaking ill of the dead in front of relatives, or it could have been to remind everyone that Linton was one who had to gain from Farold's death—for now he would be the rich but elderly miller's closest surviving kinsman.

Linton spit on the ground, looking as though he'd prefer to spit at them.

Thorne said, "Look, Rowe, let Selwyn come with us to explain for himself. Bowden is a reasonable man. But his daughter is weeping and carrying on…"

Bowden. That was Anora's father, and it was because of Anora that he was being accused, Selwyn knew. All summer he and Farold had vied for Anora's attention and affection, and in the end Anora had chosen Farold. The two youths had fought, two weeks ago, in the street, in front of everyone. Well, more accurately, Selwyn had tried to fight, and Farold—bigger, taller, stronger—had dumped him unceremoniously into the rubbish heap as though Selwyn were about ten years old, much to the entertainment of the bystanders. So now, apparently, everyone thought he had carried the fight further.

"The girl accuse him?" Selwyn's father asked, for he had never thought much of Anora. Selwyn was shocked at the idea.

"No," Thorne said. "I told you, it happened at night: Nobody saw anything. Derian didn't hear anything, what with the noise of the waterwheel and being half deaf as he is. It looks like the murderer climbed in through the window. Let the boy come and talk, Rowe. Settle this now. Do you think you're helping, acting this way?"

Finally—and Selwyn felt both relieved and terrified about it—his father nodded and stepped away from the shovel.

"Good," Thorne told him. "Fine. Now go up to the house and tell Nelda and her mother you'll be back by supper." Linton, and two or three of the others, looked ready to protest, but Thorne nodded encouragement and said, "Go on."

Selwyn's father put his arm around Selwyn's shoulder, and the two of them turned toward the house.

Whereupon they were leaped on from behind.

Selwyn hit the ground hard, facedown in the dirt with no time to get his hands up to break the fall. Somebody had a knee on the back of his neck and was yelling, "Get his hands, get his hands!"

Selwyn's hands were pulled behind his back, and someone had rope, which proved that Thorne-of-all-the-fine-reasonable-words was a liar and had been planning something like this all along.

The majority of them had gone after his father: How many men does it take to bring down a too short, too skinny seventeen-year-old who's only ever been in one fight—and lost it? But there were so many men piled up on his father, Selwyn couldn't even see him. Still, he was all right, he must have been, for Selwyn heard him cursing.

"Rowe," Thorne said, "I swear: You give us any trouble and I'll let them go ahead and club you on the head, and we'll drag you back. Selwyn's fine." Thorne looked to check only after he'd already said it, trustworthy friend that he was. "We just don't want either of you doing anything foolish. Rowe." Still Selwyn's father struggled. *"Rowe."*

In the end, they took the rags Selwyn and his father had wrapped around the shovel handles and used these as gags for both of them, replacing the taste of dirt in Selwyn's mouth with the taste of sweat and dirt.

Above the gag, his father's eyes looked frightened, and that was the worst thing of all, because Selwyn had never seen his father frightened before.

Selwyn was dragged to his feet and given a shove that wasn't as rough as it could have been—or as gentle—in the direction of the village. What about his mother, he worried, who would come looking for them when they didn't return for the noon meal?

He stopped, digging his feet into the road, anxiously looking back the way they'd come. Somebody smacked him on the back of the head, hard enough to make his knees go weak. At the same time he was shoved again. But someone grabbed him to keep him upright. They kept him walking.

TWO

✛

In the village, everyone was gathered around the house of Bowden, the headman. As many people as could fit were jammed inside, with the overflow in his yard and in the street. It was noisier than a feast day.

Thorne pushed his way indoors. Most of those who'd gone to fetch Selwyn were able to squeeze their way in, though that suddenly forced outside others who'd been there before them.

Anora, as Thorne had said, was weeping loudly, her normally lovely face puffy and red-splotched from tears. As soon as she saw Selwyn, she threw her apron up over her head—the only privacy she could get with everyone watching her—and she began rocking back and forth on her stool. People jabbed each other with their elbows and pointed. Derian the miller, the dead man's uncle, patted her leg and said, "There, there," and glared at Selwyn.

"We brought them," Linton announced, hardly necessary with everybody staring already. "They gave us some trouble." This was something else people could see for themselves, with the two of them bound and gagged, and their clothes all torn and askew, and Selwyn's father's right cheek turning purple from someone's knuckles. But Linton always tried to make himself important. He was the kind of man who would say, "Sure is raining hard," in case you hadn't noticed. And if you had, and you answered, "Yes, I can see," Linton would try to convince you that it rained hardest of all over his house.

Bowden had a fire going, an extravagance on such a warm day. But he liked to show off that he was the wealthiest man in the village, even if his house had only one room, just like everybody else's. Still, Selwyn couldn't have been the only one to find it hard to catch a fresh breath, with the wood burning and the closeness of all those people.

Bowden stood, slowly, and asked Thorne, rather than Selwyn, "So what's the boy's story?"

Why did everybody keep talking *around* him?

"Home all night with his family," Thorne answered with a slight shrug that could mean anything.

Selwyn thought at him: *Your long nose and bright eyes make you look like a rat.* This was the first time in all those years of knowing him that Selwyn thought this.

Bowden, he decided, was like a bull—lazy but dangerous.

Bowden turned those lazy, dangerous eyes on Selwyn's father, who was raging incoherently into his gag and struggling as though to burst his bindings. He asked him, "Supper till sunup: You willing to assure everybody there's no way your boy could have gotten out of the house in the dead of night, with everybody asleep?" His father nodded vigorously, but Bowden continued, "You generally keep a guard on the door, to make sure he doesn't let himself out to get into mischief?" to which there was no good answer, yes *or* no.

His father began talking into his gag again. Nobody could make out his words, but then Selwyn guessed Bowden was more interested in appearing clever than in learning facts.

"Now, Rowe," Bowden said, "nobody's accusing you of having a hand in this. Everybody knows there were bad feelings between Selwyn and Farold over my Anora."

Anora, who'd finally come out from under her apron, hid her face once more.

Bowden continued, "Young men and hot blood—we've all seen it before. I blame myself, partly, for not seeing it coming, for not forcing Anora to make her choice faster. Still, once she chose Farold, that should have been the end of it. But Selwyn wouldn't leave it at that. We all saw the fight Selwyn provoked in Orik's tavern. And once Farold beat him in that, too..."

Bowden shook his head mournfully as though to say violence wearied him, though he'd been one of the on-lookers that day, laughing and cheering, not caring who was the victor, just happy for the entertainment. "Of course, he was humiliated, only stands to reason. And it only stands to reason you want to protect him, him being your only boy and all. But, Rowe, this was no hot-tempered accident: Selwyn came up on Farold in the middle of the night, stabbed him while the man was asleep. Somebody that would do that..." Again Bowden shook his head meaningfully. "A temper like that, why, there's no telling what might set it off again."

"No!" Selwyn cried into his gag, shaking his head for emphasis in case anyone had any doubt as to what he was saying.

"Why not take the boy's gag off?" someone in the room recommended. "Hard to get a sensible answer out of him otherwise."

"Just the boy's," Bowden said.

The gag came out, leaving Selwyn's mouth foul and dry. "I didn't do it," he protested. "Yes, I was angry that Anora chose Farold. But I didn't hate him enough to kill him." Farold wasn't all that bad, Selwyn once again forced himself to think, as though this generous thought could prove his innocence. Farold wasn't as bad as a runny nose when you were trying to impress a girl. Farold wasn't as bad as a case of hives on your bottom.

Bowden narrowed his eyes. "You're not saying it's Anora's fault for choosing Farold over you?" he said.

That was all Selwyn needed—to have Bowden fearing he'd go after Anora. Why couldn't the man ask simple questions with straightforward answers? "No," he said. "I'm saying I didn't kill Farold."

Derian chose then to say, "Farold was always a good boy," which, in other circumstances, Selwyn might have disputed. Which, in other circumstances, a lot of people might have disputed. Still, with Derian, one could never be certain how much of a conversation he actually heard. But the old miller was the one who had raised Farold, whose parents had died young. So if he was distracted, there was grief as well as deafness to account for it.

Bowden gestured to someone who was standing closer to the table. An object was picked up and passed from hand to hand. "Recognize this?" Bowden asked.

Selwyn thought surely his heart was going to stop. "I—I—I—" Of course he recognized the distinctive long-handled knife—it was his own. It was a coming-of-age gift from his father, who had brought it back from his time of service in the war, and not another like it in the village. "I lost it, about the time of the harvest." He glanced anxiously around the room. "Raedan"—he had spotted one friendly face, then another—"Merton. You remember I lost it. I looked around everywhere. I kept asking if anyone found it."

"Aye," Raedan said readily, and his brother Merton was nodding, too.

Selwyn turned to Thorne—even if he did look and act like a rat—whose word should count for more, not being one of his age-mates.

And Thorne did say, "I remember."

But Bowden said, "Harvesttime was when Anora first told you she'd chosen Farold. Your conveniently losing your blade at that time shows just how long you've been planning this."

"No!" Selwyn cried. Could they misconstrue and twist everything?

Bowden handed the knife away, and it once more passed from person to person, a circuitous route back to the table, since everyone wanted to see it. "Where were you last night?" Bowden asked.

Selwyn hesitated, knowing the truth would hurt him. "Home," he lied. "Just as my father tried to tell you."

There was a reaction in the room to that: an insubstantial sigh that rippled over the crowd.

Selwyn guessed a moment before Bowden announced: "You were seen, boy."

He considered denying it, on the chance that Bowden was bluffing, or that there was only one witness, one who might not be sure, or reliable. But he'd already miscalculated and proven to those assembled that he would lie, which was a worse blow than any they'd dealt him. Aware of the pain on the face of his father, whom he had also made a liar of, he nodded. "Yes," he admitted. "All right. I was out at night. Early. But I didn't go anywhere near the mill, and I didn't kill Farold." All of which was true. "Did whoever saw me say I was near the mill?" If they had, they were lying, though he had no way to prove that. But it would be good to know exactly where he stood.

Bowden held his hand up to keep anyone in the

room from answering. "I'll ask the questions," he said. "Were you or weren't you near the mill?"

"I was not," Selwyn said. He saw Bowden was going to ask, anyway, so he told all of it, working hard to keep his voice steady: "No closer than we came today, from the farm to here."

The ripple that passed through the crowd was more distinct this time, a murmur of voices.

"Here?" Bowden asked with a glower at his daughter that said he would speak to her later, if this turned out to be true.

"I saw Anora at the market yesterday morning. She…" He hesitated, not wanting to get her into trouble; and, after all, *said* was too strong a word. "She indicated that, if I came…" He started again, hoping the words would be easier if he came at them from a different direction. "She gave the impression that… She seemed to think she might have made a mistake in agreeing to marry Farold. I thought… if I could just talk to her privately, she might break off the betrothal."

The room burst into an uproar.

"Oh, Selwyn," Anora said, her voice little more than a sigh, and immediately the noisy speculation stopped so that people could hear. "I never said that."

"No," Selwyn agreed. "But we talked, and you… you…" He thought of her sweet smile and the way she would tip her head up to look at him, for—short as he was—she was tiny. Distracted, he tried to remember exactly what she *had* said.

"I was trying to be kind," she said, sympathy in her

pale blue eyes. "You looked so sad when I told you I was to marry Farold, and then after he held you down in Orik's tavern and poured ale all over you then dropped you in the midden pile…"

Thanks for reminding me, Selwyn was tempted to say. *I'd almost forgotten how bad it was.*

Anora finished, "I was always fond of you and I didn't want to hurt your feelings. But I never said to come last night."

"No," he admitted, "but I thought…" He looked away from her, to the floor. Obviously, he had thought wrong.

Bowden said to Anora, "So did you see him last night or no?"

"No," Anora answered.

Bowden turned to Selwyn.

"I threw pebbles at the shutter over the window," Selwyn told Bowden, "but I was afraid of waking you or your wife. So I stopped."

"I must have been asleep," Anora said. "I never heard." She added, "But I believe you."

Selwyn feared she was the only one who did.

Bowden sighed in exasperation. "We don't know what time of night Farold was killed," he reminded everyone, "whether or not Selwyn did stop here first. Or after. We only know he was killed sometime be-tween supper—after which Linton left and Derian went upstairs to bed—and before Linton returned at dawn."

"Long enough for the body to start to stiffen," Linton

explained, self-importantly since he'd been the one to discover the deed, "but not to smell."

"Well, in this heat it will have started to smell by now," someone in the room commented, a loud whisper that carried.

Anora gave a wail and ran outside, the only way to get away from all the eyes that turned to catch her reaction. Her mother followed close on her heels.

"Thank you very much, Orik," Bowden said.

Orik shrugged sheepishly. No doubt he was cranky that this huge crowd was accumulated in Bowden's house, rather than at Orik's tavern—where he could have been selling food and drink to everyone.

It went on like that a little longer, people commenting and offering opinions, and few of them believing a word Selwyn said. Perhaps it would have been different if he hadn't started by lying, but there was no way to know and nothing he could do now.

By midafternoon, those few who professed to be unsure—mostly Selwyn's age-mates and, unexpectedly, Holt the blacksmith—were overruled by the majority, who proclaimed that Selwyn was assuredly guilty. Guilty because he had cause to hate Farold, because it was his knife that had done the deed, and because—even though no one had actually seen him climbing through Farold's window—he *had* been in the village at about the right time. It was enough.

The law required a life for a life, but no one in the village had been executed in living memory. Some argued that he should be sent to the bigger town of Saint

Hilda, where there was a regular magistrate who could oversee the carrying out of the sentence. But it was pointed out that the magistrate would probably demand his own investigation, which everyone agreed was pointless; and he'd want to see the body.

And that would be dangerous. The village of Penryth was too small to have its own priest and depended on the occasional wandering friar to bless weddings, babies, and the dead. But to leave an unblessed body unburied by nightfall—especially the body of a murdered man—was asking for trouble. No matter what the church said, the people knew there were night spirits eager to make a vacant body their own. Farold needed to be buried soon.

That was how they got the idea to solve two problems at once: "We will go up to the hills," Bowden proclaimed in his best official voice, which Selwyn had always thought sounded as though he had a pain in his lungs. "We will go to the burial caves, and there we will seal the dead victim in the tomb with his living murderer—Farold and Selwyn together."

THREE

"I didn't do it!" Selwyn cried, the same thing he'd been insisting all afternoon. They hadn't believed him yet, but he couldn't just stand waiting quietly while they worked out the details of how best to kill him. All that he gained was that they put the gag back on. His hands, of course, had remained tied all along.

Bowden was giving orders to tie his father to a chair, saying that he would be easier to control once all was done and over. "No harm will come to you or your wife because of your son's crime," he promised.

Someone asked how long it was likely to take—a question Selwyn was desperate to hear the answer to. But by then they were half dragging, half carrying him out the door. He didn't even get a last look at his father.

I didn't do it, he thought, just in case the fervor with which he thought it could reach his father. But surely his father already knew.

Outside, the sun was resting pink and orange on the horizon, it being that time of autumn when afternoons don't last long and there's hardly any evening at all. Torches were lit. Selwyn wondered if one would be left in the burial cavern with him. But even if he was lucky and died quickly, he would certainly last longer than a torch.

Someone had fetched a wagon—Orik's, judging by the smell of ale that had seeped into the boards from leaky barrels: strong enough that a man hardly needed to go into Orik's tavern to get drunk. Selwyn was hoisted up into the back of the wagon and laid face-down, where he'd be the least trouble to those in charge of him.

But he raised his head at a commotion, and any hope that he could make himself unaware of what was going on disappeared. A second group of people came out from the mill, carrying an ungainly cloth-wrapped bundle that had to be Farold. For a moment he thought they'd made a litter to carry the body. But as they set the corpse in the wagon beside him, Selwyn realized that the miller's nephew didn't need a litter: Death had made Farold stiff as wood—and before anyone had been able to fold his arms decorously across his chest. Selwyn closed his eyes and turned his face; but the wagon was too small to get away from Farold's outflung arm, much less the smell of him. The odor was just the herbs with which the village women had washed the body before sewing it into the shroud, Selwyn told himself. The body hadn't really begun to decay—yet. Farold wasn't all that bad, Selwyn tried to tell himself again. He wasn't as bad as…as…as a skunk dying under the porch? Bad idea, Selwyn chided himself. This was definitely no time to be thinking about dead things.

Selwyn took short rapid breaths—inhaling the smells of ale, herbs, wood, and his own sweat—and by the time they reached the hills, he was light-headed, but not enough to be groggy and confused, which would have been a mercy. Hands dragged him up out of the wagon, then turned him around and sat him on the edge when it was obvious he couldn't stand on his own.

Anora was there, crying loudly. Selwyn had been aware of the noise in the background, along with the creaking of the wagon's wheels, the *clump-clump* of the horse's hooves on the path, and—above all—the beating of his own heart. Derian Miller had come, too, "To see the boy off," he'd said, obviously meaning Farold, not Selwyn.

But when Thorne asked, "Do you want to say anything…before we lay him in?" Derian shook his head.

"Nothing to say," the miller said. "He was a good boy, with a lot of years ahead of him."

"Amen," murmured Linton, willing to take that as a prayer lest he, as another of the dead man's relatives, be asked to come up with a better one of his own.

"Amen," the rest of those assembled echoed.

Bowden, as headman, should have been there but wasn't. He had used the excuse of someone having to stay to watch over Selwyn's father, though more likely he simply didn't want to make the almost three-mile walk. Bowden was better at giving orders than at doing.

As usual, Thorne took over in Bowden's absence, having to be quick to outtalk Linton. "Anybody want to say anything on Selwyn's behalf?" he asked.

People glanced at one another uncomfortably. Nobody looked directly at Selwyn.

Linton snorted.

Holt the blacksmith said, "He was a good boy, too, till this happened."

Linton snorted again.

What a glowing testimonial. What a moving summation of his life. Even about to die, Selwyn felt a pang of indignation. If he had been really dead rather than just condemned, would his friends have been able to come up with something? *Selwyn,* they might have said.... He came back to his own earlier eulogy for Farold: *Selwyn,* his friends might have said, *he wasn't as bad as a skunk dying under the porch.*

The entryway to the burial caves was manmade: a barrow of heaped stones, blocked by a rock at least as big as Orik's wagon. It took four men, including Holt Blacksmith, to move it. Beyond lay the cave where people of Penryth had been buried for time out of memory.

A dusty, musty stench rolled out of the opening—not as bad, in the end, as Farold. But people tied cloths to cover their noses, which was not a good sign—definitely not a good sign—as two men bent to pick up Farold, and several others clustered around Selwyn, ready to guide, drag, or carry him into the barrow, whichever was necessary.

He would have walked—he wanted the men to be able to tell his family he had gone to his end with dignity—but he tried to pause for one last look at Anora, even though she was still hiding her face, crying, and they thought he was resisting. He was grabbed under each arm and pulled forward so quickly he couldn't get his feet properly under him, so that they dragged behind, and the more he struggled to right himself, the more everyone thought he was resisting.

Then they were going over the uneven ground at the entry of the barrow, and then they were heading down a steep, winding slope, the torches casting flickering shadows on the craggy walls and ceiling. The caves in these hills had been carved by nature; but men of long ago had smoothed some of the ways, though not by much. Several in the burial party stumbled or slid. And then—oh, then—the full stench of that whole villageful of dead bodies hit him. The most recent was Snell—a year dead in a hay-mowing accident with a scythe.

Bodies lay in niches or lined the walls, some set on top of one another. Wrappings had moldered or been chewed to rags, giving glimpses of withered brown flesh or bones.

For long, long minutes they walked down that corridor lined with the dead.

Selwyn heard a crunch and saw that Thorne, who

held Farold's feet, had accidentally stepped on a piece of bone. Linton, who had hold of Farold's shoulders, kicked what remained toward the wall. Something dark and furry darted out of the way and disappeared into a crack. Even if Selwyn had been walking under his own power before, that would have been enough to turn his knees to water.

The corridor continued, curving beyond them, but Linton gasped, "Enough. God, enough." And even Thorne, who normally liked to contradict everything Linton suggested, agreed.

There was a niche cut into the wall that had a pile of cloth whose flatness attested to the body inside being no more than bone. "Move that one on top of this one over here," Thorne said.

Two who had helped drag in Selwyn moved to make room for Farold, but the ancient cloth disintegrated in their hands, spilling brittle bones that shattered and scattered on the ground.

Thorne gestured that it didn't matter, that they should just keep moving, and that moving fast would be best of all. He and Linton laid Farold down in the dusty niche.

"What about him?" Linton asked with a jerk of his head in Selwyn's direction.

"Sit him down," Thorne ordered.

Someone pushed Selwyn's legs out from under him, sitting him down hard in the grit of the cave floor.

Thorne took a length of rope he'd had looped around his belt, and he tied Selwyn's ankles together loosely. Then Thorne took out his dagger.

"What are you doing?" asked Raedan.

Selwyn hadn't even realized he was there, until he heard his voice. *Don't stop him,* he thought, wanting to warn Raedan's good intentions away. If Thorne was willing to speed Selwyn's death, that could only be easier.

But Thorne said, "I'm going to cut away a bit at the rope around his wrists."

"Why?" Linton demanded.

"I'm not going to leave him tied up like this, unable to move for days."

"Why not?"

"If you don't know, I can't explain." Thorne sawed at the rope, just enough to weaken it, just enough so that Selwyn would have to work to get it off and so wouldn't be able to follow the burial party on their way out, just enough to salve Thorne's conscience.

Linton said, "Yeah, well, first thing he's going to do is take off his gag, and then we'll have to listen to him bellowing all the way back."

"Then we'll have to move out of here fast," Thorne said. "We won't be able to hear him with the rock back in place." Immediately he started back the way they'd come, those with the torches lighting the way.

Raedan paused just long enough to rest his hand on Selwyn's shoulder, then scrambled to catch up.

Linton's voice came back, whining to Thorne, "I'm going to tell Bowden."

Selwyn worked to break loose the remaining strands of rope. He couldn't escape, he knew that. But he was frantic to get closer to the entry, where the air was fresher, where there wasn't such a sense of the dead eagerly waiting for him to join them.

The glow of the torches grew smaller and fainter, and then disappeared entirely. He was in total blackness—absolutely no different from having his eyes closed. But all about him there were noises: drips and rustlings and scratchings. *Vermin,* he told himself, not an angry spirit come back to demand, "What have you done to my bones?"

He thought he heard the hollow echo of the rock rolling back over the entrance. Or maybe not. He *was* deep in the cave.

His former friends and neighbors were probably halfway down the hill before Selwyn, twisting and tugging, managed to snap the rope where Thorne had weakened it. As Linton had warned, the first thing he did was to remove the gag. He had told himself he'd be brave. He knew it was useless—even if the villagers could hear him, which they could not—but he couldn't help himself. He yelled and screamed for them to come back.

Eventually, long after his voice gave out, he was able to pick loose the knots that bound his ankles. He stood, slowly, his hands outstretched in the darkness. He shuffled forward a careful step. His hand touched something cobwebby and dusty that would have better remained untouched. To the right seemed clear. But somehow one of the broken bones was under his foot, and his leg slid out from under him. He put his hands out to break his fall and landed on one of the bodies.

Cloth and bones caved in under the pressure of his outflung hands, sending up a cloud of acrid dust. Still on his knees, Selwyn backed away hurriedly, trying desperately not to inhale. But now something was tangled up around his left ankle. His own rope? Or one that had held a corpse's blanket? Or a corpse itself?

Selwyn brushed at his ankle and stood, smacking his head. That must be where ceiling curved down into wall, which meant he needed to take a step backward. But in that direction was another body. To the left, and he banged his shin against a rocky outcropping. Once again he fell—once again on a body. This one held up under his weight. Which was a good indication it was Farold.

Selwyn let himself sink back down to the floor. He wouldn't be able to find the entry, anyway. Better to be still. Then, if some angry spirit *did* come to accuse him, he would be able to say, "It wasn't me who disturbed your rest. Go haunt those who are still alive."

FOUR

✠

Selwyn breathed through his mouth in an attempt to get away from the smell of all those dead people. But that made him sure he could taste them in the back of his throat, which was even worse.

He tried to compose himself for death, even though he knew it would be a long time coming. God knew he hadn't killed Farold, but there were other matters that weighed on Selwyn's soul and needed praying over. Like drinking too much ale that day two weeks ago, and egging Farold on to a fight, which was surely wrong—as well as foolish. Selwyn prayed to be forgiven for that, even though he felt that multiple bruises and public humiliation were surely atonement enough for that particular sin.

With his forehead on his upraised knees and his hands clasped around his legs, he also prayed for the peaceful repose of those around him. He mentally emphasized the word *peaceful*.

There was a crawly sensation on his neck that he told himself was his own mind playing tricks because he couldn't see, or maybe a drop of sweat. But it was distracting, and this was a time for wholehearted attention, and a drop of sweat was a matter over which he had control. He brushed at his neck and knocked loose something many-legged and wriggly. At least, he thought he'd knocked it loose.

He hoped he'd knocked it loose.

He beat at his chest and arms and those parts of his back he could reach.

Maybe, he told himself, *it will be easier to concentrate on prayer...later.*

The hours dragged on. Scurrying animals rustled about doing...he could only guess, and he didn't like to. So far, anyway, they seemed timid and scurried away when he flapped his arms or moved his legs or yelled at them to leave him be. Which was better behavior than he got from the noiseless insects that periodically crawled over him.

He heard bats—at least he hoped they were bats, and not restless souls. For why would ghosts who haunted these caves need to wait till actual night, when it was always night this deep in the cavern? Whatever they were—*Bats,* he told himself, *definitely bats*—there were a lot of them, fluttering their leathery wings, squeaking. He ducked and covered his head, having heard of bats getting caught in people's hair. These were cleverer than that. They swooped down and by him, missing his head by what felt like the span of only two or three fingers. They must have a means to the outside. He tried to follow them, and once more bruised his head and shins in the dark, and in the end the bats went on without him.

Hours later they returned, which meant it must be close to dawn outside. He waited, but the blackness around him did not lessen. Nor did the cold. He was so thirsty, his throat felt closed in upon itself.

The cold, at least, there was a solution for, with all those blanket-wrapped corpses near by. He preferred to stay cold.

"Peace," he assured the dead through chattering teeth. "I'll take nothing of yours."

Eventually there came a stirring that might have been the bats, though—all things considered—he wouldn't have thought it was night again already.

No, it wasn't the bats; *they* were overhead. This was something moving along the floor, at a distance but coming closer. Something that scattered pebbles as it approached. A big something. His disgust and fear of the insects and rats dissolved at the thought of bigger predators. He had wanted a quicker death than starving or freezing or lack of water, but here something was going to jump out of the darkness at him and rip out his throat, and he wouldn't even know what it was while it was killing him.

This was what he got for not praying while he'd had

a chance. He tried to make up for lost time with sincerity.

Bear, wolf, one of the big cats? Or—an even more distracting thought—a dead creature, jealous of the air he still breathed, the blood flowing through his veins?

Let it be quick, he prayed. And lastly, desperately: *I'm sorry for everything.*

There was, incredibly, a faint glow that grew brighter as the sounds of approach drew nearer. A torch? Had the villagers relented?

Suddenly Selwyn realized what had happened: They had discovered the true murderer. They had seen what an awful mistake they had made and were coming to release him, no doubt hoping desperately that they weren't too late.

Except...

Except if that were the case, wouldn't they be calling out to him, reassuring him that his rescue was at hand? Wouldn't they be eager to let him know they were coming?

This didn't sound like a crowd. This sounded like one. And not likely his father, escaped from Bowden, nor Raedan or Merton feeling sorry enough to come back for him. Any one of them, too, would be calling out.

There definitely was a light; he could see the glow reflecting off the walls of the cavern. That eliminated an animal, come to eat him, which would have been his second choice after rescue. Did spirits glow? The light was just distinct enough to give him his bearings, to show him that whatever was approaching was coming from deeper within the burial cavern.

The light came around a corner.

After a full day of total blackness, the brightness hurt, and he threw his hands up to cover his eyes, hoping if it was an angel, it wouldn't be offended, and if it was a ghost…He was very much hoping it wasn't a ghost.

He peeked out from between his fingers.

A figure dressed in black approached, its head covered by a hood. One hand was outstretched, and the light wasn't a torch after all, although it was much too bright for a candle flame. It took Selwyn several long heartbeats to realize the ball of light hovered over the outstretched palm, not attached to anything. The figure's other hand held a corner of the hood up over the lower portion of its face.

Not hiding, Selwyn realized. Protecting its nose.

Surely an angel that was set to accompany dead souls to the afterlife should be used to the smell of death. And—Selwyn forced himself to be reasonable—so should dead spirits that walked the earth.

The figure had stopped. It was standing directly in front of him, looking down at where he crouched on the floor among all those long-dead and not-so-long-dead bodies.

The hand holding the hood dropped, revealing a long strand of white hair and the face of an old woman. This old woman said, "Truly you look terrible and smell worse. But whoever buried you obviously knows nothing about dead people."

Which didn't sound like something either angel or ghost would say.

He swallowed convulsively, though there was absolutely no moisture in his mouth. "Are you—" He had to stop, his throat constricted by thirst and terror.

"Carefully now." The old woman raised a warning finger to demand his attention. "Ask something foolish, and I *will* have to smack you on the side of the head." She emphasized this, as though they'd already discussed it.

His voice creaking with dryness, Selwyn asked, "Do you warn me beforehand what questions are foolish?"

Apparently not. And apparently that was one of them. She smacked him on the side of the head.

"Ouch."

"Well, I warned you," she said.

He decided not to risk asking her anything else. He would have backed away, if there was any place to back away to. All he could do was huddle miserably on the floor.

"Foolish questions," the old woman explained, "are things like 'Am I dead?' or 'Are you dead?' or 'Are you a ghost?'"

They all sounded like reasonable questions to him.

Perhaps she could see he thought so, for she looked prepared to smack him again.

To distract her, he asked, though it hurt his throat to speak, "What if I asked you then: 'Who, or what, are you?' I'm not asking who or what you are," he hastened to add. "I'm asking: 'Would it be a foolish question to ask you: Who or what are you?'"

It took her a few moments to work that out. In the end, she smacked him again, but he saw it coming and ducked, so she only clipped his ear.

"That was for the 'What are you?' part. What could I possibly be, in a place such as this, with a light such as this, seeking something from the dead?"

Selwyn gulped, although she was right. It was obvious. She was a witch.

The old woman continued. "But I didn't smack you for asking *who* I am, for there's no way you could know that. My name is Elswyth." She hit him again.

"What was that for?"

"That was for not asking for water, which you obviously are in desperate need of." She set the glowing light on her head—or, rather, a handspan above her head—and unfastened what he had thought was her humped back. It was, in truth, a pack. The light dipped to follow her as she sat down on the floor, more limber than he would have guessed from her age. She searched through the bag and pulled out a wineskin, which she handed to him. It held water, musty and warm and more wonderful than anything. The inside of his throat unstuck from itself, but he didn't want to appear greedy and selfish—not to a witch who could balance a ball of light over her head and who had an inclination for hitting. "Thank you," he said, offering it back still half full.

"Go ahead and finish," she said. "It's plain water. I haven't bespelled it."

It hadn't occurred to him to worry that a witch might give him water tainted by witchcraft. Until she said it.

He finished the water anyway, for whatever harm there was in it was already done. "Thank you," he said again, much subdued.

"You're welcome."

He glanced around the corpse-lined cave and both wondered about and flinched from the thought of what she might want from the dead.

Elswyth took pity and answered the question without making him ask it. "For one of my spells, I need a lock of hair from a man newly dead. I heard that someone had died in Penryth on the other side of the wood, so I came to the burial caves." She glared at him through narrowed eyes. "I hope you're not the one they were talking about. You won't do at all. *Did* somebody think you were dead?"

"No," Selwyn assured her. "Farold is the dead man." He waved in the general direction. Farold had most definitely begun to smell, a sickly sweet odor from off to Selwyn's right. "I'm here as punishment for killing him—*not,*" he added in the same breath, "that I *did* kill him. But I was accused of it." He didn't know what to make of the look Elswyth was giving him. Did she believe him? Or, considering that she was a witch, would she prefer to hear that he really was a murderer?

She said, "So your townsfolk accused you of murder and condemned you to die here alongside your victim?"

Not knowing where—if anywhere—lay hope of rescue, Selwyn nodded.

Elswyth said, "Sweat from the brow of a condemned man is an ingredient in several spells. May I?...in payment for the water I gave you? I very much believe in payment for favors granted." She was already rummaging through her pack.

Selwyn looked at her in horror. She didn't care: Murderer or innocent victim of justice gone awry, it made no difference to her. He was sweating despite the cold as she took a piece of unbleached wool from her pack and blotted his forehead with it.

"Good," Elswyth said. She folded the cloth and placed it in a small wooden box. "Fine. This will do. Now shall we discuss what you'll pay me for leading you out of here? I assume you *do* want to leave—unless you are so overcome by feelings of guilt that you believe you deserve to die this way."

"I told you," Selwyn said, "I didn't do it."

She waited, without reaction, for his answer.

"Of course I want to get out," Selwyn said. "I'll do anything you want if you'll help me."

She smacked him on the side of the head. "That," he heard her say once the ringing in his ears began to fade, "is for being too foolish to bargain. So be it. You owe me a year of your service: housework, chopping firewood, fetching ingredients for my spells, whatever I ask. For a year."

"No," Selwyn said, suddenly realizing what he might have gotten himself into.

"Too late. You already agreed beforehand. You're lucky I'm in a good mood and didn't say you owe me your entire life." She shook her head. "Foolish boy," she muttered, getting to her feet. "How was an old woman like me to keep you from following me out anyway, for free?" Just the thought of how foolish he'd been drove her to hit him again.

Selwyn saw it coming, but—seeing how foolish he'd been—he didn't even try to duck.

FIVE

✛

The witch Elswyth took a knife from her pack and once again held the edge of her cloak up over her nose. She sniffed. Once was enough to find Farold. All Selwyn's flailing about in the dark—walking into walls and risking the ire of the spirits of the dead that he stumbled over or into—had taken him fewer than a dozen steps from where the burial party had originally left him.

"Wait," Selwyn whispered in horror, looking at Farold's dangling arm. "He moved."

Elswyth sniffed again. She told Selwyn, "*You* smell terrible. *He* most definitely smells dead."

Which didn't ease Selwyn's fear at all.

Seeing his face, Elswyth snapped impatiently, "He's not moving."

"I don't mean now." Selwyn wasn't willing to come any closer. The magic light that hovered over Elswyth's head was bright enough to leave hardly any shadows, which was both fortunate and not. "But…" He pointed first at the body, shrouded in one blanket, then at the arm, which had a separate wrapping, for Farold had already begun to stiffen before the village women prepared him for burial. It was one of the last things Selwyn had seen, as the torches were being carried away: Farold bundled into the niche in the wall, his arm sticking straight out. But now it hung down, still wrapped, the edge nearly brushing the floor.

Did I break his arm? Selwyn thought, horrified, recalling how he had walked into Farold's body in the dark. Would Farold's spirit be restless because of it?

Would Farold's spirit be *angry* because of it?

Surely not as angry as it would be at whoever had killed him, Selwyn assured himself. Surely a man who had gone through murder wouldn't hold the accidental breaking of an arm against someone.

Elswyth shook her head at him, as though all his thoughts were written on his face. If she had been standing close enough, she probably would have smacked him yet again. Pressing the cloth of her cloak even tighter against her nose, she used her knife to cut open the seam the village women had sewn to close Farold into the blanket. She wrinkled her face on seeing the two-day-old corpse, which made Selwyn think better of her. Then she picked up the dangling arm and folded it over Farold's chest, as if she, too, believed in decorum. "Dead bodies go stiff," she told Selwyn. She wiggled the loose arm. "And then they relax again. There's nothing to fret about here, except that in another day the body will start leaking, and we'll want to be away by then."

And except, Selwyn thought squeamishly, that she seemed to have more experience than anyone should with dead bodies.

She leaned over and cut off a lock of Farold's light brown hair, then wrapped it in another piece of unbleached wool cloth from her pack. Finished, she tucked the blanket back under Farold's body as carefully as a mother tucking in a sleeping child.

"I'm finished here," she told Selwyn, "unless you wanted to steal some of the knives or rings or other possessions these people were buried with."

"No," Selwyn assured her hotly. But then, for the first time, he considered that perhaps not all her suggestions were meant to be taken seriously. "No," he repeated more calmly.

And she did smile.

"Come." She swept the light from its place a handspan above her head so that it once more rested not quite in her palm. "Your service to me begins now. You will start by carrying my pack."

"Elswyth," he called. It seemed overfamiliar, considering the vast difference in their ages, considering the power she had. But he wasn't sure how one addressed a witch. Obviously not *My lady. Your Unholiness?* But she had given the name Elswyth, whether or not that was truly her name.

She turned back to look at him, with an expression that didn't seem annoyed with his familiarity but that warned she was prepared for—and willing to deal harshly with—any nonsense he might be planning.

He spoke quickly. "I'm worried about my family."

She glanced around the burial cavern. "Are they here?" But her tone was suspicious.

"No," he said hurriedly, before she became too distrustful of anything he said. "But they know I was put here."

Elswyth obviously didn't see the connection. She gestured for him to continue speaking, motioning with the hand that the light followed, which was dizzying to watch.

"They won't realize that you've…" He hesitated, then said, "rescued," and she snorted. He took a deep breath. "They won't realize that you've rescued me." He drifted off, unsettled.

"Then they'll have a pleasant surprise a year from now, won't they?" she said in a tone that hinted she didn't entirely believe that would be the case.

Selwyn spoke quickly, for she'd started to turn back around. "But my father…I'm worried about my father. That he might do something hasty and foolish. That he might try to rescue me himself, or go after Bowden, who sentenced me to this fate. And then they might do the same to him, or kill him outright."

She was regarding him blankly.

"I'm worried that if my father doesn't know I'm safe,

he may do something rash that will endanger his own safety."

Elswyth said, "Are you trying to ask something?"

She was a witch, Selwyn reminded himself. Despite the fact that she looked like somebody's grandmother, she was not used to the love and concern of families. "I'm asking if my service to you can begin tomorrow. I'll carry your pack out for you," he assured her hastily. "I'll accompany you wherever you want to go. But I want to stop by home first, and let my parents see I'm unharmed, and let them know I'll be coming back in a year."

"But you won't," Elswyth pointed out. "For surely your villagers would take your continued existence badly."

"Oh." Selwyn was embarrassed he hadn't thought of that. "Then, I'll tell my parents that I'm unharmed, but that, obviously, I won't be able to return home. They'll be satisfied with that, if they have to be, so long as they know I'm safe."

Elswyth was shaking her head. "If *you* suspect that your father might attempt rescue or vengeance, surely others will have the same thought. They'll have set up a watch on him."

The hard part was knowing she was probably right.

"Then," Selwyn said desperately, "can *you* send word to them?"

"Would that be before or after your father tries his rash scheme and is punished for it?"

"Well, what do you suggest?" Selwyn cried out in frustration.

"That you let the world take care of itself," Elswyth said.

"We're not talking about the world," Selwyn said. "We're talking about my family."

Elswyth looked at him with that face of hers that gave away nothing of what she was thinking.

Selwyn tried to control his ragged breathing. "I need," he said, "to prove that I didn't kill Farold. That's the only way I'll ever be able to return. That's the only way my family can ever go back to being what it was."

Elswyth's eyebrows went up skeptically, but she didn't contradict him. "What are you asking?" she asked.

"I'm asking that the year I promised to give you be delayed, until after I've proven my innocence."

"And what are you offering in return?"

Selwyn tried to evaluate her, as she so clearly kept evaluating him. "More time?" he asked hesitantly.

"Another year," she agreed.

Selwyn's heart sank. But if he could survive a year in her service, surely he could survive two.

Elswyth said, "You will give me two years of service for delaying the start of that service until tomorrow morning."

"Tomorrow morning?" Selwyn squeaked.

"You asked for tonight."

"But that was to explain to my parents," Selwyn said, "not to undertake to prove my innocence."

She held out her arms to show she was being open and generous. "How long? If you never succeed, does that mean you will never fulfill your obligation to me?

There must be a time limit, after which you will come to me whether you have achieved your quest or not." Selwyn was about to say he supposed that was fair, when she said, "One week. In exchange for one more week of freedom, you will give me a third year."

"But—"

"If you haven't accomplished what you propose in one week, what makes you think you'll ever be able to? If you feel, at the end of that week, that you are close to proving your innocence, come speak to me about it, and we'll see what can be arranged."

Selwyn had a vision of the entire remainder of his life spent in her service.

"Agreed or not?" Elswyth asked.

"Agreed," Selwyn said, for he had no choice. "Except—"

This called her back as she was once again beginning to turn to leave.

Elswyth sighed loudly, as though she was the one who kept losing in this bargaining. "What?"

"What would it cost me to buy a spell from you?"

Selwyn didn't at all like the smile she gave him at that.

"What kind of spell?" she asked.

"A spell to prove my innocence."

"You will have to be more specific than that," she told him.

Selwyn considered. There were only two people who knew for a fact that he was innocent: he himself and the murderer. He cast a nervous glance at Farold's shrouded body. Well, actually, counting the dead man, that made three. He swallowed hard and said to Elswyth, "You know a great deal about dead bodies."

"I'm well read," she told him with a wildly innocent smile.

"Do you know how to bring the dead back to life?"

"No," she said. But she paused to deliberate. Selwyn held his breath, which had nothing to do with the smell. She said, "Well, perhaps. But only temporarily. And it depends..."

Selwyn could hardly get his voice to work, knowing he was getting himself into the darkest sorceries. He asked, "On what?"

Elswyth counted out on her gnarled fingers, having to go around the magic light. "The right ingredients. Which, by coincidence, I do happen to be carrying with me." She moved on to a second finger. "The amount of time the dead has been, in fact, dead." She, too, glanced at Farold. "Which, in this case, may be a complication." She moved on to her third finger. "And the willingness of the dead to come back."

Selwyn said, "I will give you yet another year of my life to raise Farold from the dead for me, just long enough so that he can publicly proclaim that I didn't kill him."

"Oh, no," Elswyth said, almost laughing at how ridiculous that offer was. "The casting of this spell will cost you three years all of itself, whether your Farold chooses to heed its call or not."

Three years! Selwyn thought. Without assurance that it would work. On top of the one year he had already agreed to for Elswyth's showing him out of the cavern, and another for not starting his service immediately, and...He said, "If Farold clears my name tonight, I won't need the extra week we discussed."

Elswyth gave that smile he was growing to dread. "But you already agreed."

Selwyn gritted his teeth. *Six years.* But what other choice had he? He nodded.

Once more Elswyth put her magical light over her head to free her hands. "Bring the body here," she commanded Selwyn.

"You mean, touch him?"

Elswyth smacked him on the side of the head. "If you tell me that you can magically transport him without touching him," she said, "I'll apologize for that."

Selwyn took many gulps of air, and flexed his fingers, and closed his eyes and wished that he would awake from this terrible dream. But in the end he had to walk over to where Farold's body lay, and he had to get his hands under the weight of it, and he had to pick it up—all loose and floppy as it was.

"Don't worry," Elswyth said, "he won't start to fall apart for several more days."

Selwyn began to gag, though he hadn't eaten since earliest morning a full day and a half ago.

Elswyth pointed to another body, set in the wall and resting on a litter. "Bring me some of the wood from that one's bier."

It would do no good to protest. Dry pieces broke off easily in Selwyn's hands—this body had lain here a long time. Selwyn whispered an apology to it, anyway.

"Kneel down," Elswyth said, "and don't break the circle."

"What circle?" Selwyn started to ask, but Elswyth was already scratching a mark on the rocky floor with a sparkling stone she had gotten from her pack, a circle that was big enough to enclose her, Selwyn, and Farold, as well as the wood he had brought. Next, she arranged this wood into a neat little pile, and she set about trying to strike a spark, using flint, steel, and a bit of flax.

"Can't you start a fire magically?" Selwyn asked.

"One can't use magic to make magic," Elswyth told him. "And every time you speak, you drain energy and make the spell weaker."

Selwyn wasn't convinced she didn't say that only to keep him quiet, but he stopped asking questions, just in case.

Once Elswyth got a fire going, she pulled a little clay pot from her pack and placed that on the heat. She emptied two vials into the pot: one a clear, bright red liquid—*like melted rubies,* Selwyn thought; the other a thick blackish purple substance that she had to shake out of its container. It made a rude sucking sound when it finally wriggled out, then landed with a noisy *plop* in the already-simmering red ingredient. There was a loud *hiss,* a blue cloud of smoke, and a nasty smell that momentarily made Selwyn forget the smell of where he was.

Elswyth unwrapped Farold's blanket again and cut off another hank of his hair.

His skin had an awful greenish cast. Without even

realizing it, Selwyn slid backward on his knees. Glow-ering, Elswyth grabbed hold of his wrist before he broke the circle. She had talked of the dead person's willingness to come back, and Selwyn had been amazed, assuming any dead person would be glad to be alive again, even temporarily. Now, seeing the state of the body they were asking Farold to come back to, Selwyn wasn't so sure.

Elswyth placed Farold's hair into the pot, along with various leaves and powders from her pack. Lastly she pulled from her pack a human leg bone, dry and white. She waved this, wafting over Farold the still-blue smoke from the clay pot, and began to call Farold's name.

Selwyn was light-headed, even without the smoke.

In a low singsong, she apologized for disturbing Far-old's rest and told him that his friend—which Selwyn had never been—needed him. "You died an untimely death," she chanted, "cut short, unfairly, unfairly. Your grieving friend seeks your aid to unmask your mur-derer."

She tipped Selwyn's head, forcing him to look at Farold, which he'd been steadfastly trying to avoid. She handed him the bone, setting the other end down on Farold's forehead. "Come back," she said, which Sel-wyn imagined she meant for Farold, even though she was looking at him. She gestured, and he realized he was to repeat her words.

" 'Come back,' " he squeaked.

"Use these ingredients...," Elswyth said, wafting the smoke.

"'Use these ingredients...,'" Selwyn echoed.

"And my strength..."

That explained why she was having him help. But Selwyn repeated the words: "'And my strength...'" Was it just his imagination, or did he really suddenly feel weaker? There was no other choice, he reminded himself.

"And enter into this body," Elswyth finished, gesturing for him to make sure the bone stayed touching Farold.

"'And enter into this body.'"

But at the very moment Selwyn spoke, there was a sudden noise in the cave, a commotion. His body jerked involuntarily, ready to fend off attack.

It was only the bats, once more stirring as, outside, daylight faded and nighttime settled. In a moment Selwyn had recovered from his start, but then one of the bats—so clever and agile the night before—fell into his lap.

"Ahh!" Farold's voice screamed, small and many octaves too high. "What have you done?"

Selwyn looked down at the bone Elswyth had handed him, which he'd unwittingly raised off Farold's brow, and which—even now—was pointing straight up, up to where the cloud of bats above swooped and swarmed and flew beyond the curve of the corridor, deeper into the cavern. Leaving one behind.

Elswyth reached over Farold's perfectly still corpse and over the bat that fluttered and raged and tried unsuccessfully to right itself. She smacked Selwyn hard. "Fool!" she cried.

SIX

✛

The bat was having trouble standing upright. Unable to get its balance, it kept flapping its wings, but this caused it to rise slightly off the ground, at which point it would squawk, stop flapping, drop back to the floor, and tumble over. Then start all over again.

"Fool?" the bat repeated after Elswyth, its voice tiny but definitely Farold's. *"Fool? Fool* doesn't say the half of it!"

Selwyn offered a steadying hand to keep the bat from tipping over.

In appreciation, the creature kicked him. But then it began hopping about, one tiny foot lifted, yelping, "Ow, ow, ow, ow, ow! You big bully!" It tried to kick Selwyn with the other foot, and flopped onto its back.

Selwyn held out his finger, and the bat reluctantly took hold and pulled itself upright, using the tiny little thumb at the edge of its wing as a hand. Selwyn looked from the bat with its huge ears and large fleshy nose to Farold's corpse, to Elswyth. "What happened?" he asked helplessly.

"*'What happened?'*" the bat shrieked. "*'What happened?'* What kind of fool question is that? Selwyn Roweson, you dumb twit, even *you* should be able to see *what happened.* You dumb twit." Still holding on to Selwyn's left forefinger, it kicked at the bone in Selwyn's right hand, missed, and found itself—both feet off the ground—dangling by its thumb from Selwyn's finger.

Elswyth, naturally, sided with the bat. She snatched the bone from Selwyn and shook it at him. "Didn't I tell you to keep this pointing at the corpse?"

"Well, actually," Selwyn corrected, "you didn't so much tell as show—"

She smacked him on the head with the bone.

"Yes," he agreed for safety's sake. "Yes, you did."

"Then why did you go and point it at the bats?"

"I didn't do it on purpose," Selwyn said. "It was just, the bats made a sudden noise that frightened me."

"Frightened you?" both Elswyth and the bat shrieked at him. Elswyth pointed the bone at the tiny bat and yelled at Selwyn, "Look at him. He's about as big as your finger. What, precisely, do you find so terrifying that you had to go and muddle the spell?"

"The *noise* startled me," Selwyn protested. Why did she always make things out so that he sounded like a fool? "I wasn't frightened of *one* bat." He decided against mentioning that the whole swarm of bats was a little more intimidating than one all by itself. Most likely Elswyth wasn't intimidated by any number of bats, and she looked ready to use the bone on his head again. He said, "So Farold's spirit returned to the wrong body? It went into this bat's body? Can we redo the spell?"

"No," Elswyth said in a tone that indicated, once again, he was a fool. And, to Farold, she said, "Bats can't stand, so stop trying."

"As though it's not bad enough being dead," the bat complained, still clutching Selwyn's finger and jumping up and down with rage, "now I've got to be a rodent, too?"

"I'm sorry," Selwyn said.

"Actually," Elswyth said, looking thoughtful, "you're not."

Selwyn and the bat looked at each other. "Who's not what?" the bat demanded. "He's not sorry?"

Elswyth shrugged. "That I have no idea about. But you're not a rodent."

"I'm a bat."

"That's a different thing entirely. Bats have mouse-like faces, but they're in a completely different order from rodents."

"Thank you very much, professor." The bat spit on the floor. "Now there's a thoroughly useless piece of information to add to this whole mess. I *look* like a rodent, I *feel* like a rodent—who are *you* to tell me I'm *not* a rodent, you ugly old witch?"

Selwyn saw the flash of irritation in Elswyth's eyes.

He pulled back his hand so that the bat could try to escape, but it stood its ground, wobbly but defiant.

Elswyth raised the bone, which was big enough to send the bat—or Farold, or Farold in the bat's body—back to where she'd just summoned him from. But she took pity on his small size and, instead, hit Selwyn.

"No wonder someone murdered you," she told Farold as Selwyn rubbed his leg but didn't dare complain that this latest attack had been unfair. "You're a very irritating little snippet."

The bat stood motionless for a moment. "That's right," it finally said, much subdued. "I *was* murdered. That was how I came to be dead. I remember hearing you call me, and that's why I came back."

"Right," Selwyn said, glad to be back on the topic they needed to be on. "We called you here so that you could tell us who did it."

The bat that was Farold said, "I thought you called me here so that *you* could tell *me*."

"*What?*" Elswyth snapped.

"You don't know who killed you?" Selwyn asked in horror.

"I was asleep, you dumb twit. It was the middle of the night, and it was dark, and"—the bat beat at Selwyn's hand with its wings, as though forgetting that it *had* wings, and not hands—"if you had looked before starting all this, you would have seen that I was stabbed *in the back*."

Selwyn rested his forehead on the palm of his hand.

Elswyth threw down the bone, too disgusted even to hit him.

"As much fun as this has been," Farold announced, "seeing you act the fool again, Selwyn, meeting the old witch here, I think I'm going back now. The afterlife makes a lot more sense than you do."

"Wait!" Selwyn cried. Six years. He'd just given away six years of his life—to be insulted by Farold, hit by Elswyth, and end up no further ahead than he'd been when this had started. "But you *did* want to find out who murdered you. That's why you came back, you said."

"For all I know, it could be you," Farold said.

Elswyth gave a cry of exasperation. "What is it— something in the water that makes everyone in Penryth fools? Why would he have paid to bring you back if he was the one who killed you?"

Farold didn't ask what he had paid. "I suppose," he agreed.

"So the real murderer is free, and I've been blamed," Selwyn said. "And Bowden condemned me to die here in this cave with you."

"I don't think Bowden is going to release you on my say," Farold said, flapping his bat wings. "He'll be con- vinced this is some kind of trick. Either that, or he'll have you up on charges of witchcraft."

Selwyn didn't argue, because he was thinking how *he'd* react if an accused murderer came bearing a talking bat that claimed to be the dead man. Instead, to show Farold there was benefit in this for him, too, he said, "But if you help me, maybe the two of us together can find out who did it, and you can rest easier in the afterlife."

"I *was* resting easy," Farold grumbled, "until you disturbed me." But then he said, "All right, why not? Besides, I'd like to see Anora one more time."

At the mention of Anora's name from those little bat lips, Selwyn felt... he wasn't quite sure what. It wasn't a good feeling, whatever it was: a bubbling of jealousy, anger, guilt to be pleased that Farold was now, obviously, no longer competition.

Elswyth smiled sweetly and took her revenge on Farold for his earlier unkind remark. She said, "Then I suppose it's a good thing you're in the body you're in. A three-day-old corpse makes such a poor first impression."

"Ugly old witch," Farold repeated.

Looking from Farold to Selwyn, Elswyth said, "The two of you deserve each other."

SEVEN

Selwyn rewrapped Farold's corpse, Farold finding
fault and nagging all the while, complaining, among
other things, that Selwyn wasn't doing the job with a
properly respectful attitude. It was hard to look respectful while fighting the urge to vomit. Selwyn re-
solved that henceforth he would try to avoid situations
where he had to prepare a corpse while the corpse was
in a position to criticize.

He set the body—with its arms now folded properly
across its chest—back into the wall niche, which
he thought meant they would be ready to leave the
cave.

Apparently not.

"What?" Farold demanded. "No prayer?"

Elswyth sighed—loudly—but waited.

Selwyn gave Farold what his uncle Derian had spoken at the cave mouth: "He was a good boy, with a lot of years ahead of him."

"That's it?"

Selwyn was ready to cope with annoyance. But Farold sounded so dejected, Selwyn didn't have the heart to point out that he'd done a fairly good imitation of Derian. Nor did he think it appropriate to say: "Here lies Farold. He wasn't as bad as a skunk dying under the porch." Instead, he said only, "It's distracting, with you standing there listening."

"I'll be happy to help," Elswyth offered, "when we set you down for good."

Farold didn't take amiss what sounded, Selwyn thought, much like a threat.

Still, even then, leaving wasn't easy. Farold, in the bat's body, had as much trouble flying as he had had trying to stand upright.

"Let the bat's mind take over," Elswyth recommended. "*It* knows how to fly."

"*It* doesn't have a mind to speak of," Farold said. "*It* only wants to go outside to eat bugs with the rest of the swarm."

"'*Swarm*'?" Elswyth repeated contemptuously.

"Flock, herd, whatever a gaggle of bats is called."

"Colony," Elswyth said. "A group of bats is called a colony. I was about to say you're thinking too much, but never mind."

"Eat bugs and leave droppings," Farold scoffed. "Big thinkers."

"Hang upside down by their toes," Elswyth added, making a lunge for him.

Apparently the malice in her tone and the sudden movement frightened Farold enough that the bat's mind was able to take over. He fluttered up to Selwyn's shoulder, leaving—as he had said—bat droppings along the way.

Selwyn didn't protest. He was in no humor for anything that would delay just getting out of the cave. "You can practice once we get outside," he told Farold. And, to Elswyth, "It's all right, I'll carry him."

"You'll carry the pack, too," she reminded.

Selwyn reached down to pick up the pack, which was heavier than he had anticipated, and bulky. He needed a moment to swing it across his back and adjust the ropes across his shoulders—which made Farold grumble at the inconvenience of having to move to his other shoulder—and by then Elswyth had started without him.

"Don't lose her," Farold complained. Everything Farold said came out sounding like a complaint.

"Oh," Selwyn said, as though the thought had never occurred to him. "All right then."

Farold missed the sarcasm and just muttered, "Dumb twit."

Elswyth led them deeper into the cave, the light above her head bobbing with her quick sure steps. The awful smell lessened, for the bodies this far in had rested here a very long time and were mostly dust. The way narrowed and became even more twisty.

And then Elswyth ducked her head and stepped

sideways through a crack, and her magic light winked out.

"Now you've done it," Farold told him.

There's nothing worse than a traitor, except a traitor with a bat's night vision: Farold lifted off his shoulder and abandoned Selwyn to the dark.

Selwyn hurled himself at the crack. He could feel it with his fingers, but even when he turned sideways as Elswyth had done, he couldn't fit through.

The pack, he realized; it was the pack that was bumping against the wall, blocking him. He swung it off his back and held it in his right hand, edging his left shoulder into the crack. He scuttled sideways, feeling rock at his back and his front. There was no time to delay for panic at the prospect of getting wedged between immovable rock: He was sure Elswyth would never have the patience to come back for him. Two shuffling steps. Three. And then the walls of rock were gone, both the one his back was scraping against, and the one before his face.

He was still in darkness, but he could make out shadows, and darker shadows, which meant more light than there had been before. Best of all, the air was crisp and clean, smelling of fallen leaves and apples. He tipped his face upward and saw pinpricks of light.

He was outside, looking at the night sky.

Elswyth smacked him on the back of the head. "Are you going to stand there all night gawking at the stars?"

She couldn't ruin his mood. *He was outside.* He wasn't going to die after all. Or at least not within the next day or so. Or at least not that he knew of. And, anyway,

it wouldn't be all alone in the dark, surrounded by
those who had gone before him.

He was outside.

And even the fact that there was no sign of Farold
couldn't diminish that. He trusted that Farold would
have the sense not to wander far.

"This is very inconvenient, you know," Elswyth told
him, taking the pack, as though she hadn't carried it all
the way here without him, as though she hadn't been
in the habit of carrying it herself before she met him.
With her finger she traced a circle on his forehead.
"Seven days before the circle closes," she said, using
the voice that he already recognized as her voice of
power. She walked around him, her finger still touching
so that she made another circle, this one going around
his head, from his forehead, over his right ear, around
the back, over his left ear, back to his forehead. "Seven
days, then you will be drawn to me." She moved the
finger down, over nose, lips, chin, and neck, then off to
the left, where she made a circle over his heart. "Seven
days, and you will have to come to me." She laid her
palm over his heart.

Selwyn felt the beat alter, the rhythm shifting—he
suddenly knew without knowing how he knew—to
match hers.

She withdrew her hand, adjusted the backpack, and
started walking.

"Wait," Selwyn called after her. He'd never been
here before, on the far slope of the hill that held the
burial cave; he'd never heard of this second entrance.
But he could get his bearings by the tall hill that was

called the Grandfather because it somewhat resembled the profile of an old man with a beard. "Penryth is that way."

"*Go* that way," Elswyth called, without even looking back. "Come to me in seven days."

So she wasn't going to stay to get him out of any trouble he might get himself into: He could have guessed that. "But I don't know where you live." Selwyn took several steps to keep her within hearing. "Beyond the wood, did you say?" Not that that helped: The whole area was heavily wooded. The only witch he had ever heard of nearby was in the village of Woldham, but that one was tiny and stooped and gnomelike, by all accounts, and had only one good eye. Elswyth, though white haired and wrinkled, stood tall and straight, and he hadn't noticed that either of her eyes was cloudy.

"*In* the wood," Elswyth corrected. She turned then to look at him. "You will find me." She gestured toward him, then toward herself, resting her hand against her own heart. Selwyn's heart did an odd, almost-painful flutter. "In seven days, you will be drawn to me irresistibly. You will be unable to *keep* from finding me."

She let her hand drop, and Selwyn's heart stopped its frantic racing, his head cleared of the buzzing that had suddenly filled it, the muscles in his arms and legs stopped throbbing, and he could catch his breath.

Elswyth turned once more, and Selwyn would have let her go, but something smacked into the back of his head.

"I just can't manage those landings," Farold said.

"And gnats and midges taste terrible. Have you ever tasted gnats or midges? Why couldn't you have made me a fruit-eating bat? What's the plan? Are you going to let her go before you have a plan? That doesn't sound very smart to me. What if you need her magic again, and you've gone and let her go?"

Finally, someone had said something that got Elswyth's attention. "*Do* you need another spell?" she asked, coming back.

Selwyn could guess where *that* conversation was heading. "No," he assured her.

"Yes," Farold said, settling once more on Selwyn's shoulder.

Selwyn snapped at him, "You want to deal with her, you make your own arrangements."

"*I* don't need her magic," Farold said. "*You* do." Before Selwyn could object, Farold continued, "I can walk—so to speak—right into Penryth, and not a person is going to recognize me. Is that your plan? To have me listen outside people's windows and hope to overhear someone saying to himself, 'Ho hum, last Tuesday I murdered Farold and nobody knows it. What will I do for fun next Tuesday? Maybe I'll murder Bowden,' and then I can tell Bowden that whoever-it-is is going to murder him and we can lie in wait and catch him trying, and then he'll admit to killing me, and so everyone will know you weren't the one, and you can come back? Is that your plan? Because as soon as anybody sees *you*, how do you think they're going to react? *I* think they're not going to listen to a thing you have to say, and they'll decide they can't risk putting you back in a cave you obviously are capable of getting out of, so they're just going to go ahead and stone you or burn you or chop off your head—which they may or may not get right the first time, since they don't have any experience at it."

Elswyth said, "The bat makes sense."

"Well, that wasn't my plan," Selwyn said.

"What is?" both Elswyth and Farold asked together. Selwyn tried to think.

"He needs a disguise," Farold said.

"*That* doesn't have to be magic," Selwyn said.

"Where are you going to get a disguise without magic?" Farold asked. "And how are you going to be sure people don't see through it unless she magically changes you?"

"Fine," Elswyth said. "For another year."

"I didn't say *yes*," Selwyn protested quickly.

"I suppose you could go back in there"—Farold waved a bat wing back toward the burial cave—"and get different clothes by stripping one of the bodies. And maybe somebody was buried wearing a hat, and you could pull it down over your face and hope nobody wonders why."

"Six years, seven years," Elswyth said. "Not that much difference. But I don't have all night for you to make up your mind."

Selwyn hated being rushed.

"Maybe you could shave your head," Farold suggested. "Do you think anybody would recognize you if you shaved your head? Not that I have a blade, of course, excepting the one in my back if no one removed it. But someone probably did, or my body wouldn't have lain flat. I could pull your hair out, one strand at a time."

"I *do* have other things to do," Elswyth said. It seemed as though they were determined not to give him a moment of silence to think. "I'm gathering supplies for a very important spell. If you delay me too much longer, I may get grumpy and raise the payment to two years."

He was being pressured into a too-hasty decision, Selwyn knew it.

"I have an idea," Farold said eagerly to Elswyth. "You could make the two of us look like wealthy merchants from the East. Give us silks and jewels and gold."

"I am not," Selwyn said, "giving up a year of my life so that you can try to impress people with fancy clothes."

"Fine," Farold said, "have her disguise *you* as a wealthy merchant, if you think no one will wonder why a wealthy merchant is carrying a *bat* along with him."

Elswyth settled the problem. "I couldn't disguise you as a person anyway," she told Farold. "You're a *bat*. You're this big." She gestured with her two hands not very far apart. "There's not enough of you to stretch out"—she spread her arms—"to human size."

"Hmpf," Farold said.

Elswyth looked at Selwyn. "I could make rich-looking clothes for you, but I can't actually make you rich."

And what would a richly dressed merchant be doing,

all alone, without any merchandise, in a small village like Penryth? Selwyn said, "Why don't you just give me different clothes, different color hair..." He gestured helplessly.

"Different eyes," Elswyth finished, "bigger nose, smaller mouth..."

Selwyn nodded.

"For a year's service?"

She was determined, he realized, not to give him the excuse that he hadn't actually accepted her bargain. "For a year's service," he agreed.

"People will get suspicious if you have a bat with you," Farold warned.

He just wanted a disguise, Selwyn thought. "Let them get suspicious," he said. If he was lucky, maybe somebody would catch Farold and wring his neck.

EIGHT

✦✦✦

Selwyn asked for pilgrim's clothes, which made Farold—who'd been incessantly whispering into his ear, "Rich merchant's clothes"—cry out in disgust and flutter away. But Selwyn felt his choice was sensible. In all of his life, he had rarely seen strangers. Penryth was too small to attract newcomers; and it wasn't on a trade route, so even people passing through on their way to someplace else were infrequent. Most of the strangers he *had* seen had meant trouble: renegade soldiers, bandits who occasionally turned up in the most heavily wooded section of the road to Saint Hilda's, the two feuding wizards—banished from the king's court for incompetence—who had been competent enough to nearly level Orik's tavern. But Selwyn remembered that when he was a child a small group of pilgrims had traveled through on their way to the shrine of Saint Agnes of the Lake. They'd worn rough-spun robes and sandals, and those who'd been on pilgrimages before had badges and emblems and necklaces of seashells to show where they'd been.

Now at the last moment he thought to ask, "And could I be a clean pilgrim, please?"

Elswyth said, "Pilgrims aren't known for cleanliness."

"They're cleaner than this," Selwyn said, mightily aware that he stank. He had gotten used—he had thought—to the smell of death. But now that he was out of the cave and within hope of once more in his life being clean, the lingering smell of death on him was becoming intolerable. "A little road dust is fine."

"We need water for the spell, anyway," Elswyth told him.

He didn't like the grin that thought brought.

The hills saw the start of several streams, which twisted and converged and eventually formed the river that turned Derian's mill wheel. Elswyth rejected two before finding one that looked especially deep and swift moving. "This will do," she said.

Selwyn eyed the steep and slippery-looking bank, thought he knew what was coming, and held his tongue. This lasted only until, rummaging through the contents of her pack, she ordered him, "Fetch a stick."

"From the water?" he cried.

Elswyth looked up at him. "If you really want," she

said. "Myself, I would try to find one on the ground, or break one off one of those trees or bushes over there."

Farold swooped out of the dark to mutter, "Dumb twit," then snapped up a moth and disappeared back into the night.

The moon was bright enough to see by, even when Selwyn stepped out of the circle of Elswyth's witch light. He found a stick. In fact, he found several, and he brought them all to her—short, long, thin, thick, straight, gnarled—having no idea what she needed it for. Not a fire—for she'd definitely said *one.* He guessed she'd find all of them lacking and would call him a fool.

But she hardly glanced at them and only said, "Take one in your hand."

"Which?"

Then came the look that indicated he was a fool. She gestured impatiently. "Any."

He held on to one and let the others drop.

She must have had an endless supply of wool squares, for she took another one from her pack and placed it on his head. "*Now,*" she told him, "you get to go in the water." It was no use protesting. He knew he winced, but she continued, "Go into the stream, sit down, lie down—whatever is necessary to be totally covered by the water—hold on to the stick, hold on to the wool, count to five—" *That* gave her a moment's hesitation. "Do you know how to count?"

"I can get to five," Selwyn assured her, stung. A farmer needed to be able to count at least well enough to time things.

"And then come out again," she finished.

He was sure at least half of this was simply to torment him.

The stones on the edge of the stream were wet and flat and very slick. He almost slipped twice, jerking and flapping his arms and scrambling with his feet, but still keeping hold of both stick and wool head-covering. The third time he wasn't as lucky. The cold water closed in at about waist level—leaving him momentarily breathless.

"That isn't deep enough," Elswyth called, as though he was stopping there, as though he didn't know the difference between the water being up to his waist and the water covering his head.

He got up and waded to about midstream, but the water didn't get much deeper. He had to sit in it, and it still didn't cover his head, so finally he had to lie back in the water, and then it closed over his face.

Onetwothreefourfive, he mentally counted in the space of about one heartbeat. But he didn't want to have gone this far for nothing—to have her send him back, saying, "Do it again, slower." So he counted more slowly on his own, pausing between each number. *One. Two. Three. Four. Five.*

Except she had said, "Count." Now he suddenly wondered, *Did she mean count out loud?*

Sure he was going to be the death of himself, Selwyn counted out loud. His pace was faster than his second mental counting, but slower than his first. "One, two, three..." By the time he reached "four," he was out of breath, the air gone out of him in the same bubbles that carried his voice. He just barely managed "five," then sat up, gasping, hating himself, hating Elswyth, wondering how she talked him into these things.

He got to his feet, leaning on the stick, which—surprisingly—didn't break under his weight, and which—amazingly—was tall enough to support him even standing. He looked down and saw that it had become a thick, smooth walking staff. His clothes had changed, too: Shirt and breeches had become a brown rough-spun robe, and under his hand the square of wool had changed shape and material. He lifted it and found a straw hat.

"Get out of the water before you get soaked," Elswyth yelled at him.

And, incredibly, he realized that the part of him that was out of the water was totally dry. He made his way to the bank, and the water that had covered him ran off, the way water runs off metal.

"I thought you said you knew how to count to five," Elswyth berated him. "You stayed in there so long, I thought you'd drowned."

She didn't, he noted, say anything about being worried, or about coming in to get him. He didn't explain that he'd become confused about her instructions but only said, looking at the hat and staff, "I didn't understand about the cloth and the stick."

"Magic can't make something out of nothing," Elswyth said. "That's why I said I couldn't give you gold. What—did you think I was just being difficult?"

Selwyn decided it was safest not to answer that question. He saw that the hair on the back of his hands was thick and dark, and that his hands were much broader than they had been. The dunking she had inflicted on him had changed his appearance, as well as his clothes, making him stocky rather than just small, and darker, and—he felt his face—hook-nosed. He said, "Thank you. This will work out well."

"I doubt that," she snorted.

Farold landed on his shoulder. "The pilgrim and his bat are ready," he announced, "and doesn't that make a foolish-looking picture? A pilgrim and his dog makes much more sense."

"Six months for a dog," Elswyth said, making the offer to Selwyn—since he was so lucky—and not Farold. "And it will be a small dog."

"A bat is fine with this pilgrim," Selwyn said.

"Then I will see you," Elswyth said, "in seven days. Actually, now that you've wasted so much time, six and a half."

She didn't even wish him luck.

NINE

✛

Elswyth went, and finally there were no more reasons for Selwyn to call her back. He wavered between relief and alarm: relief because he no longer needed to protect his head and arms from her attacks and because he was in no more immediate danger of bargaining away more years of service to her; alarm because he was on his own. Being with Farold was no discernible improvement over being alone.

He gathered what wild berries he could find in the dark, which left him still starving but no longer faint with hunger.

"What are you doing?" Farold demanded in his irritating little voice as Selwyn began to look for a comfortable place to sit—to, perhaps, catch a little sleep.

"Looking for a place to rest until morning," Selwyn said. He'd spent the last two nights in a mass grave, sleeping fitfully when exhaustion got the better part of terror, so he wasn't fussy; he settled down on a grassy area and tossed away only a couple sharp-edged rocks.

"Oh, that makes sense," Farold told him. "Pay the witch by the hour, then first thing you do is take a nap."

"Excuse me," Selwyn said. "You've been comfortably dead for the past three days. I've had to live through them."

"Dying takes a lot out of you," Farold argued. "I won't even mention the strain of some dumb twit bringing you back as a bat. Let's see if you do better when it's your turn to die."

Selwyn was uncomfortably aware of just how close he'd come to having it be his turn. Rather than quarrel with Farold, he explained, "But I can't just walk into Penryth in the middle of the night. You know them. They'd be convinced I was a thief or ruffian of some sort and run me off for sure."

Farold didn't say anything—which likely meant he agreed but didn't want to admit it.

Selwyn said, "This will give us the opportunity to talk."

"I'm not allowed to tell about the afterlife." Farold took hold of a nearby branch and hung upside down from it. "That's one of the conditions, before people are allowed to leave."

"All right," Selwyn agreed slowly. Now that he

thought about it, he couldn't believe that he'd spent all this time with someone who had actually died and come back, and never once had he wondered to ask what it had been like—a question that had nagged at people throughout the ages. He had been too caught up in his own concerns. Farold gave him a self-satisfied, self-important smirk—Selwyn could recognize the expression even on bat lips, even on bat lips hanging upside down in the predawn dark. "All right," he repeated, disappointed—now—that he wouldn't be able to ask the questions he had previously not thought to ask. He went back to what he'd been going to say. "Then let's talk about your enemies."

"I don't have any. Everybody liked me."

"I didn't," Selwyn pointed out. "And somebody killed you. Or did you stab yourself in the back? Was it suicide after all?"

"*I* didn't like *you,* either," Farold snapped. "I'm constantly reminded why."

"This bickering is getting us nowhere. Who would have wanted you dead?"

Farold, upside down, shrugged.

Selwyn said, "I think it could have been Linton."

"Linton is my cousin," Farold protested. "Why would he want me dead?"

Selwyn refrained from saying, "*Because* he's your cousin," and instead said, "To get the mill." Linton was the oldest of Derian's sister's children, and for the past two years he had been helping at the mill.

"Then he would have killed Uncle Derian, too." Farold seemed suddenly to realize the full implication of this. "Will he? Do you really think he killed me? Do you think he plans to kill Uncle Derian?"

For the first time, Farold sounded concerned about someone other than himself. "I doubt he would kill Derian," Selwyn reassured him. "That would be very obvious. People would suspect him if *both* of you died suddenly."

"But he could wait two or three years," Farold said, getting into the full spirit of suspicion, "and then kill him."

"If he waits two or three years, Derian is likely to die on his own," Selwyn said, "old as he is."

"Well, you certainly are the personable one, aren't you?" Farold snapped. "Don't you ever worry about other people's feelings?"

It was hard to think of a sarcastic little bat as having feelings. Selwyn told himself he would have done better and been less blunt if Farold had been in his old shape. "Sorry," he said.

"My uncle Derian raised me, you know"—Farold continued complaining—"from the time I could barely walk or talk—when my aunt Sela said her hands were already full with Linton."

"Sorry," Selwyn repeated. "I didn't mean anything." He didn't bother to point out that Farold must have been awfully slow if he was just barely walking and talking when his parents had died. Selwyn and Farold were the same age, which would have made Farold five the night part of the old mill burned, killing Earm

Miller and his wife, Liera, and their three older children. Selwyn and his family could smell the smoke from their house, seven farmsteads away. Derian had not only raised Farold, he had been the one who had rescued him from the flames. "I wasn't thinking," Selwyn said.

Farold snorted. "For a change."

Selwyn wondered how to get the conversation back to where it needed to be.

But while he was still working at it, Farold said, "If Linton killed me—which I don't think he did—but if he did, how would you go about getting him to admit it?"

Speaking slowly, still working it out as he spoke, Selwyn said, "Well, someone saw me in the village after dark. Maybe someone saw Linton, too."

"Linton *lives* in the village," Farold was quick to point out. "With his parents and his three brothers and two sisters."

Selwyn could just hear him rolling his little bat eyeballs. Did he have any idea how lucky he was that the branch he hung from was out of easy reach? "Yes, but Derian says the three of you had supper together, and then Linton went home. Maybe someone saw him come back out again, later, and return to the mill."

"And whoever saw this didn't think to mention it before—when you were being condemned to death— but they'll tell it now?"

Selwyn squirmed under Farold's sarcasm. "Before," he said, "everyone was so convinced *I* killed you, they might not have thought to mention Linton's activities."

"Oh, very likely. That explains everything."

The infuriating thing was that Farold was right. "And," Selwyn continued, "I need to find out who had opportunity to find or steal my knife."

"Your knife?"

Selwyn thought Farold's voice sounded odd, and he glanced over.

"I was killed with your knife?"

Was Farold going to need to be reassured all over again that Selwyn hadn't been the one to kill him? "Yes," Selwyn said.

But all Farold said was "Oh."

"What?" Selwyn asked suspiciously.

"I had your knife," Farold admitted.

"What?" Selwyn repeated.

"Don't take that tone with me," Farold warned, sounding much the same as Selwyn's mother would when she said the same thing.

Selwyn refused to be drawn into that argument. "Don't talk to me about tone when you stole my knife."

"I just meant it as a joke," Farold said. "Can't you take a joke? I would have given it back."

"A joke would have been giving it back after a day. You had it for three weeks."

"Yeah, well...," Farold said, but obviously couldn't think of anything else to add. He readjusted his wings. "This isn't getting us anywhere," he sniffed.

Selwyn *still* wanted to shake him until his eyeballs rattled. He took two deep breaths and gritted his teeth. "Did anybody know," he asked through his teeth, "that you had the knife? Like, for example, Linton?"

"No," Farold said slowly, thinking, "not Linton. Merton."

"Merton?" Selwyn repeated in amazement. Merton was brother to his best friend, Raedan—and also a friend. Or, at least, Selwyn had thought he was a friend. It was bad enough realizing that—all those days he'd been frantically searching for the missing knife—Merton had known where it was. That made him as bad as Farold. But worse yet was what had happened at Bowden's house: when, under Bowden's questioning, Selwyn had explained that he'd lost the blade, and Merton had agreed that this was so. And never a mention that Farold had had the knife all along. Not even when Bowden pronounced that the knife being missing for so long proved that Selwyn had been *planning* to murder Farold.

"Merton knew you had my knife?" he asked, just to make sure he was understanding correctly. "All along?" It couldn't have been all along.

"He was the one who found it," Farold said. "You dropped it that day everybody was helping Snell's widow with the hay mowing. Merton found it in the grass after we'd finished eating, and we thought it would be a good joke, after you'd been showing off with it, as usual—"

"I...," Selwyn protested, interrupting. But he couldn't deny it. He *was* proud of the knife his father had brought back from the wars. He *did* have a tendency to take it out whenever he had an excuse to show off the elaborate handle, the finely wrought blade of high-quality steel that honed to a much sharper edge than the villagers' common blades. Instead, he asked, "Did Raedan know, too?"

Farold shrugged. "I didn't tell him. But maybe Merton did. We were tired of hearing you brag about it," he finished. "I said I'd keep it because we both knew if Merton had it, he'd never be able to keep a straight face once you started asking. But I would have given it back."

"Did he know where you kept it?" *Merton?* he thought. *Merton, and maybe Raedan?*

Farold gave a leathery shrug of his wings. "I don't think I ever specifically said," he told Selwyn. "But it was in my clothes chest—easy enough to find."

"I don't think a man goes into another man's room intent on killing him and only then thinks to start looking for a weapon."

"Why would Merton come into my room intent on killing me?" Farold asked.

"Why else would he come in, in the middle of the night, quiet enough not to wake you?"

"We don't know that he did." Farold was raising his voice, just as Selwyn was. "I thought you said it was Linton who killed me."

"I don't know," Selwyn shouted at him. "I don't know who did it. I said it *might be* Linton. *Maybe* it was Merton. Maybe it was somebody else. *I* wasn't there, too stupid to wake up from being murdered: *You* were." It was hard to think of Merton as a murderer, but then it was hard to think of him as a thief—or, at best, as a trickster who was willing to let the trick go on even as Selwyn was being left in the cave to die.

"Well, don't take your bad temper out on me," Farold said. "I'd rather eat bugs than take this abuse." He fluttered off into the night, leaving Selwyn truly alone.

TEN

When Selwyn awoke after a few hours of fitful sleep, he was surprised to find Farold had returned and was once more hanging upside down from his branch. After last night, he wouldn't have been surprised to find himself abandoned.

Selwyn drank from the river and found a few more handsful of berries, but the season was nearly over and most of the berries were withered and brown and did little to satisfy his hunger. And in all this while, Farold hadn't budged. "Farold," he called.

Farold continued to hang, his wings wrapped around himself.

"Farold, time to go."

No reaction.

Maybe he had decided to return to the afterlife, as he had threatened. Or maybe the bat body itself had died. Where would *that* leave Farold?

Alarmed, Selwyn poked at the tiny form, which shuddered and pulled its wings tighter—proving it was alive, anyway. "Go away," Farold mumbled sleepily.

Selwyn leaned in closer, so that he could simultaneously poke a second time and yell into the bat's enormous ears: "Farold, you lazy lout! Wake up!"

The bat snarled at him, showing an incredible number of tiny but very sharp teeth.

Selwyn jumped back, but the bat didn't lunge. It once more closed its eyes.

"Farold," Selwyn urged. "It's morning."

"I know," Farold said, never opening his eyes. "Bats are nocturnal."

"You're not a bat," Selwyn tried to reason with him. "Not really."

"Tell my body that. Besides, I was up all night."

"So was I."

"Maybe some fool has turned you into a bat, too," Farold said. "Maybe you better check."

Selwyn shook Farold's branch. Farold's tiny clawed feet held on. He opened one eye to glare at Selwyn. "Go away," Farold told him. "Come back at sunset."

"I'm not going to waste a whole day waiting for you." A whole hard-earned day.

"Then go without me," Farold said. "You were the one who *had* to have a nap last night when it was a sensible time to get started. Don't talk to me about lazy."

"We agreed," Selwyn said, which they hadn't—not exactly—"that it was no good going at night. The villagers would have run us off."

"You can't fight instinct," Farold said from around a yawn.

Selwyn didn't dare leave him. Farold might not be able to find Penryth on his own. Last night, at the beginning, he hadn't known that bats can't stand; he had barely been able to manage flying. Things would have to look disconcertingly different for someone who only recently found himself merely a finger's length long and traveling by air. But how did one transport a bat who wasn't up to transporting itself? Elswyth hadn't given him any sort of pack—apparently she had judged a pilgrim should travel light. He certainly didn't want to carry Farold in his hand all the way. Looking around, he saw the straw hat Elswyth had made from one of her squares of wool. Carrying Farold in the crown of the hat would be only marginally better than carrying Farold in the palm of his hand. He said, "Well, as long as you're going to hang on to that branch, could you just as well hang on to the brim of my hat?"

Farold once more opened one sleepy eye. "That would look silly," he pointed out.

"Do you have a better idea?"

Farold sighed. Selwyn put on the hat. Farold let go of the branch and fluttered to take hold of the back edge. He was hardly any weight at all, dangling back there. "I told you to have her make me into a dog," he said.

Selwyn circled around Penryth to go first to his own home. He had no idea how he would explain what had happened and convince his family that he was really himself, but he couldn't bear the thought that they were imagining him dead or, worse yet, in the process of dying.

As he approached, crossing their recently harvested field, he saw no signs of activity, not even smoke from the kitchen fire. A few chickens scratched in the yard, ignoring him.

He opened the door and called in, "Hello."

The only answer came from the direction of the back of his hat. "Can't you keep it down when normal people are trying to sleep?" Farold muttered.

Selwyn refrained from saying that Farold hadn't been normal even when he was alive.

He stepped into the house and immediately saw that no one was home, not even his grandmother, who rarely moved from her favorite place by the edge of the hearth. The room was not in disarray: The floor was well swept the way his mother always kept it, the beds made, the table cleared, the benches where the family sat for meals neatly tucked beneath the table where they belonged. Selwyn poked at the ashes in the hearth and found them completely cool. No one had cooked here this morning and then let the fire go out. That might mean that they had left yesterday or earlier—but he didn't think that was likely: No matter how angry they were at the villagers for sentencing him to death, they couldn't just leave a working farm and assume they would be able to start again someplace else. More likely, someone had decided that his family shouldn't be left alone, not while there was still a chance of his not being dead yet, for that might lead them to plotting to get him out of that cave.

Surely, he told himself, *surely they are well and safe.*

He found food: more evidence, if he had needed it, that his family hadn't deserted the farm, for no one sets off just as winter is lurking around the corner and leaves good food behind. There was half a loaf of bread, so hard he had to dunk it in water to get it soft enough to eat—indication that it had been sitting here since about the time he had been taken. There were also fruits and vegetables that he ate unprepared and raw until finally, finally, his stomach was full again.

"Hey!" a voice bellowed from behind him—not, this time, Farold.

Selwyn whirled around and found Merton standing in the doorway.

"What are you doing here?" Merton demanded.

"What are *you* doing here?" Selwyn countered, remembering the business with the knife.

Merton narrowed his eyes at him. He'd been carrying a rake—*their* rake—over his shoulder, but now he swung it out in front of him, its sharp metal tines pointing at Selwyn.

He can't recognize me, Selwyn reminded himself. *He sees a stranger—a stranger who's in a house that doesn't belong to him, eating food that isn't his.*

Trusting Farold would have the sense not to speak, Selwyn lowered his gaze, to look meek and not out for a fight. He said, "Begging your pardon. You frightened me half out of my wits. I'm just a poor hungry pilgrim who got separated from the rest of his company. I've been wandering, lost, for the better part of two days. This was the first house I've seen, and I came to beg food. I didn't see that anyone was here."

Merton didn't say anything, and Selwyn couldn't tell how reasonable he found the story.

"I'm sorry," Selwyn said—as a pilgrim, there was no way that he'd know this wasn't Merton's house, so he pretended he thought it was—"I'm sorry I took your food. I'd be happy to do work for you, to make it up to you." It would, in fact, be a good excuse to stay, to find out more about what had happened the night of the murder.

Merton slowly lowered the rake. "It's not my house," he said, which was a relief: Selwyn had recognized the possibility that the farm might have been taken away from his parents, for having a murderer for a son. Merton added, "I'm just looking out after the animals..."—he hesitated—"while the owners...are away. For a day or so."

The animals. Of course, the animals would need tending. Selwyn realized the chickens would have rushed right up to him at his approach if they hadn't eaten in days. If the goats had been left loose without food, they would have wandered off for good; and if they weren't loose, they would probably be close to starving by now. "Thank you," Selwyn said earnestly. "That's very good of you."

Merton, who had no way of knowing why this pilgrim should be so grateful for his care of somebody else's animals, frowned in puzzlement.

"I...ah...have vowed to offer a prayer at the shrine of Saint Agnes of the Lake for all the good people I meet along my journey."

Which wouldn't include you, Selwyn mentally added. *Take care of my animals, but leave me to die.* He gave Merton a bright smile.

Merton said, "Well, the people who live here are good people, too. Offer up a prayer for them, and I'm sure they wouldn't begrudge you the food."

"*Do* they need prayers?" Selwyn tried to sound innocent. "Especially?"

Merton looked surprised but only answered, "Doesn't everyone?"

"Who are they?" Selwyn asked. "Where are they?"

Merton narrowed his eyes suspiciously again. "Ask a lot of questions, don't you?"

Selwyn said, "I'd like to thank them. I'm sure what I ate here today saved my life."

"*I'll* thank them for you," Merton told him. "I'm here much of the time, my farm being the next one over."

It wasn't, but perhaps Merton was only suspicious that he was a thief and was warning him that the place would be well watched. Selwyn hoped he hadn't looked too surprised, for neither pilgrim nor thief would know that Merton had lied.

"Well, God bless you and the people who live here," he said. "May each of you be rewarded for your actions as you deserve." The second part, at least, he could say in all sincerity.

Merton scowled, which Selwyn thought might be evidence of a guilty conscience.

Then again, it might have been because he caught sight of the back of Selwyn's hat as he passed—with Farold the bat hanging from the brim.

ELEVEN

✦

"Oh, that was well thought out and skillfully done," Farold told him as they headed down the road to the village. "Learn a lot, did we?"

Leave it to Selwyn's luck that Farold couldn't have slept through that ill-handled exchange. "Be quiet," he grumbled. He glanced behind to see if Merton was making sure he was really leaving and saw that he was. Merton was watching him while raking the patch of garden his mother kept, which would yield vegetables till the first frost if kept clear of leaves and debris. *That might make up for giving my knife to Farold to teach me a lesson,* he thought, *but it won't make up for not speaking up when that knife turned up IN Farold.* Merton stopped raking and glowered. Selwyn waved, lamely, which couldn't have done anything to allay Merton's suspicions that he was a thief.

"So who are we going to interrogate next?" Farold asked from his position on the back of Selwyn's straw hat.

Selwyn decided he wouldn't let Farold's persistent belittling undermine him. "Give me your advice, oh wise bat," he said.

Farold considered. "I could really use a drink."

Selwyn stopped, took hold of the hat, and swung it around so that Farold hung, upside down and swaying, in front of his face. "Don't even think about it," he warned. The idea of a drunk bat was enough to send shivers up his spine. The idea of this particular bat drinking too much—and who was to guess how much was too much for a bat?—was enough to leave him breathless.

"You look as though you could use some of Orik's ale yourself," Farold told him. "It might get rid of that nasty twitch you've developed in that one eye, and maybe even make you better company." Before Selwyn could get his mouth open to answer, Farold continued. "Besides, what better place than a tavern for people to gather and discuss one another and one another's business?"

Selwyn thought about it. "Maybe you're right that the tavern would be a good place to get information," he conceded. "But—first of all—I have no money. And—secondly—what am I going to do: Walk in there and say, 'My bat and I would like a drink of ale, please'?"

"Pilgrims are always begging," Farold pointed out.

"Not this pilgrim," Selwyn snapped.

"*Hmpf,*" Farold grumbled. "Well, thirdly, I wouldn't want to share a drink with you, anyway."

But they did go to Orik's tavern, because Selwyn didn't know what else to do.

And there they found Selwyn's father.

Selwyn stopped dead in the doorway.

His father was in the same position as when he'd seen him last: tied to a chair, though that had been in the middle of Bowden's room and this was in the corner of Orik's tavern. At least the gag was gone. He sat slumped, looking simultaneously angry, sad, and very, very bored.

"Keep moving, keep moving," Farold muttered into his ear.

Selwyn wasn't sure whether Farold, once again dangling from behind, was urging him forward because he couldn't see and was still hoping for a drink, or if he was looking where they were going, had caught sight of Selwyn's father, and was hoping Selwyn wouldn't say or do anything to give themselves away.

Selwyn kept moving, once again because he didn't know what else to do.

There was no sign of his mother or grandmother. In fact, except for Orik himself, his father was the only other person in the room.

Orik, who'd been sitting at one of the tables, looking at least as dejected as Selwyn's father, jumped to his feet. "At last!" he cried. "A customer!"

Selwyn forced himself to look away from his father. There was no way his father could recognize him in this magically made disguise—and even if he could, Selwyn didn't *want* to be recognized, for that would be the end of everything, with Orik to witness it. So he looked at Orik, and let Orik's words make their way from his ears to his mind. "Oh," he said, "no. I'm afraid not. I'm just a poor pilgrim passing through, without any money, willing to do work for a bite to eat and a corner to sleep in for a day or two."

Orik had begun wiping the table the moment he'd seen Selwyn, even though the table was already spotless. All the tables were spotless. The floor was spotless. The walls were spotless. Selwyn had never seen the place look so clean. But at Selwyn's words, Orik flung down his cloth. "Do I look as though I need to hire help?" he demanded. "To serve the crowds? To keep them from pushing and shoving to hand me their money?"

"Ahm...," Selwyn said. His gaze strayed back to his father, which wasn't necessarily a bad thing. There weren't men tied up in the corner of every tavern, so anybody would be curious.

"Yes," Orik said, seeing where he was looking. "You've identified the problem exactly." He went to one of the barrels, pulled out the plug, and poured a mug of ale. Selwyn thought he heard Farold licking his little bat lips, but Orik himself drank it down in one gulp. "Who wants to come in here, lay down good money, and look at a face like that?"

Selwyn's father glowered, and Selwyn said, "I...," and gestured helplessly.

"Exactly," Orik said, and poured himself a second mugful.

"So why is he here?" Selwyn asked.

"Because there's no place else to keep him."

"I see," Selwyn said, which a real pilgrim wouldn't have—couldn't have—from Orik's disjointed complaints. Selwyn realized he couldn't sound too knowledgeable or Orik would become suspicious. So he asked, "What's he done?"

Orik became suspicious, anyway. "If you're just passing through, you don't need to know."

"No," Selwyn agreed. Still, he tried to catch his father's eye, to indicate—somehow—that he was sympathetic, but his father wasn't looking at him.

"Go on, now," Orik told him. "I can't afford charity now."

But before Selwyn could leave, the tavern door opened. Selwyn hoped the arrival of someone to wait on would improve Orik's temper, but Orik—who'd looked up eagerly—said, "Oh, it's you."

"You" turned out to be Thorne. He came in, saying, "Just wanted to check on Rowe."

"Of course," Orik said. "Why else would anybody come in here?"

Thorne paused to glance at Selwyn. Selwyn read disapproval in his look, but at least nothing of recognition. Selwyn supposed there was much in his pilgrim's appearance to disapprove of—especially around the area of his hat, at which Thorne most definitely gave a second hard stare. But then the man turned away and asked Selwyn's father, "Everything all right? Need anything?"

Selwyn's father looked at Thorne stonily.

"Nelda will be bringing you your dinner soon," Thorne continued, just as though he'd been greeted pleasantly. "I just passed by Bowden's and saw her packing it up."

Selwyn's father still said nothing, though Selwyn was relieved to learn that his mother, apparently, was staying with Bowden's family. His grandmother was probably there, too, for she could be difficult, and few would be willing to take on her care.

"Need to use the bucket?" Thorne asked.

Still Selwyn's father said nothing.

Thorne stooped down to examine the knots of the ropes that held him. "Not much longer," he said.

"That's supposed to make me feel better?" Selwyn's father asked in a growl.

Which told Selwyn they were waiting for a day beyond which he couldn't be expected to have survived. He had guessed it already, but it was a difficult thing to hear.

Now Thorne had nothing to say. He tried to lay a friendly hand on Selwyn's father's shoulder, but Selwyn's father shrugged it away.

"Hey!" Orik shouted. "Hey!" He swatted at the air around his head. "What kind of vermin you bringing in with you?"

Thorne looked around. Selwyn did, too, though he already had a good guess what was going on—and the name of his guess was Farold.

Orik was dancing around running his fingers through his hair—not that there was that much of it—and patting his clothing and shaking out his apron and looking up, down, and around. "Something just flew off him and right into my drink," Orik explained, presumably so Thorne wouldn't think him possessed. "For four days nobody comes in here except you and Nelda to visit Rowe, and now I get somebody with flying, ale-drinking vermin."

Selwyn decided to play the innocent. "What?" he said blankly, still looking around, not letting his eyes rest on Farold, whom he spotted hanging from the shelf on which the ale barrel rested, lapping up the drops of ale that dripped from where Orik had replaced the plug.

Thorne was looking at Selwyn with the expression of a man who's just bitten into a sour peach. He asked Orik, "You mean that nasty, disgusting thing he had hanging from his hat?"

Farold made a noise of protest, drawing Orik's attention.

"Hey!" Orik said once again, sighting him.

"My hat?" Selwyn said, trying to sound simple and harmless. He took the hat off and turned it in his hands as though examining it. "I don't see anything wrong with my hat."

Farold was dipping and swooping and making *woowhup* sounds Selwyn was fairly certain no species of bat ever made.

Orik went after Farold with a broom, but—looking at where Farold was going rather than where *he* was going—he tripped over a stool and lost hold of the broom, which went flying and would have struck Thorne except that Thorne had the sense to move backward. The only problem was that Selwyn's father's chair was there, and Selwyn's father *couldn't* move backward. He and his chair and Thorne all spilled onto the floor, joining Orik.

The door opened as someone new came in, and Farold darted out with a flourish of one wing that Selwyn was sure was the bat equivalent of thumbing his nose.

"Are you all right?" Selwyn rushed to help his father, ignoring Orik and Thorne—coming close, if truth be told, to stepping on Thorne to get to his father.

Lying on his side, his father was straining against the ropes that held him, obviously hoping they'd been knocked loose.

Thorne pushed Selwyn out of his way and worked to right the chair, and suddenly Merton was there helping him—he was the one who had just entered. Selwyn had seen him duck to avoid Farold and hadn't even noted who he was.

"What's going on here?" Merton asked as Thorne made sure the ropes were still secure.

"I don't know," Orik grumbled. He was standing in the doorway, still brandishing his broom, looking right and left as though expecting more unwelcome airborne visitors. "This jackanapes comes in asking all sorts of questions, infested with some pestilent monstrosity that attacked us."

"Monstrosity"? Selwyn thought.

"He was asking questions over at Rowe's house, too,"

Merton said. "Made himself right at home before I got there. I followed him to see what mischief he was up to."

Selwyn tried to look innocent, though the act hadn't worked yet.

His father looked at him, really looked at him for the first time. Selwyn hoped Elswyth had done as good a job with changing his face as she had done with changing his clothes.

"Rowe's house?" Thorne repeated.

Orik, still on the lookout by the door, said, "Probably some kind of trained, flying, killer creature from France or someplace."

"It was a bat," Merton informed Orik. To Thorne, he said, "Think he's one of Rowe's kin? That they got word to that they needed help?"

"There was no opportunity," Thorne said. "Besides, Rowe doesn't have any kin. And besides *that*, look at him; he doesn't know him."

Selwyn's father had been studying him as though trying to figure out who he could possibly be, but now he made his face blank so that Thorne couldn't get anything from him.

Thorne finished, "He's just some clumsy, dirty, busy-body pilgrim."

Selwyn was stung. The *clumsy* one was Orik, and the *dirty* part was due to Farold—who'd left bat droppings all over his back and shoulders after Elswyth had specifically cleaned him up. *Busybody* he couldn't argue with.

"Well," he said before they changed their minds and

decided to tie *him* to a chair, "since there's no work or hospitality here, I'll be on my way." *One year,* he thought. *I paid one year for this disguise, and I've learned nothing.*

He put his hat back on his head, straightened his pilgrim's robe, and left the tavern.

Behind him, he heard the door open.

"And keep your filthy French rodent with you," Orik shouted after him.

Selwyn would have called back, "Bats aren't rodents," but he guessed Orik probably wasn't really interested. He kept on walking, aware that Thorne and Merton had come out to stand next to Orik, to make sure he truly left this time.

As he passed Bowden's house, he spied Farold, trying to catch a glimpse of Anora through the window. But when Farold saw that Selwyn was leaving, he swooped down and grabbed hold of the front of his hat so that he dangled in Selwyn's face. "Excuse me if I'm acting a little silly from being overtired," he said. "I warned you bats are nocturnal."

"Drunk," Selwyn corrected, furious but quiet so his voice wouldn't carry to the villagers who stood by the road watching him. "You're drunk, not tired."

Farold shrugged, closed his eyes, and almost immediately began to snore.

TWELVE

Selwyn was no better off than he'd been last night, when he'd decided he had no choice but to have Elswyth magically change his appearance. No matter how far he walked, all he could figure was that he had chosen the wrong disguise. He fought the idea of yet another disguise, berating himself for a fool, urging himself desperately, "Think!" Seven years he had bargained away already. He thought back to when he'd been ten years old, to fix in his mind exactly what seven years was. A big difference, that between seventeen years old and ten. He tried to think ahead to twenty-four and couldn't.

He walked and walked, knowing he eventually had to go back to Penryth, and knowing he couldn't go back as the pest-laden, suspicion-raising, troublemaking pilgrim. Yet he could no more think how to alter his magically created disguise than he'd been able to think how to make his own disguise last night.

There was no way around it: He needed Elswyth's help.

He stopped and took a shaky breath. *I will not fight it,* he thought. *One year more on top of all the rest means nothing.*

Well, not *nothing.*

He took another deep breath, and this one was steadier.

The first thing he needed was to find Elswyth. But before he could do that, he had to determine where *he* was. He had been walking for quite a while now without paying attention, concentrating on his thoughts; and somehow or other he'd wandered off the road and was in a meadow.

The sensible thing to do was to try to find the road again, to go back up into the hills, to the back entrance of the burial caves, where he had last seen Elswyth. Once there, if he was lucky, he would be able to track her.

Not that—as a farmer—he'd had that much experience in tracking.

The sun was low in the sky after a late start and time wasted, and he realized that soon it would be the hour for bats to start stirring. With that thought, Selwyn hoped one bat in particular would wake up with the pounding headache it fully deserved. Still, that was not the important thing. The important thing was that almost one entire day had passed since he'd made his bargain with Elswyth: one day out of the week that she had allotted him. Gone. To no effect. That didn't bear thinking about. Neither did the fact that—even assuming he could again find the place where they'd parted—he'd be trying to track her at night.

What else could he do?

From where he stood in the meadow, there was no sign of the road, no matter which direction he looked. He turned around, for the reasonable thing was to go back the same way he had come, assuming the road had to be nearby, assuming he couldn't have been walking long over rough ground without noticing. And assuming he had walked more or less in a straight line.

But he stopped after only three or four steps.

Somehow that didn't feel right.

Silly, he chided himself, and took another step. He couldn't bring himself to take another.

He turned again, to the way he had been inadvertently walking—the one way he knew for sure was not the way he had come.

You're wasting time, he told himself. Never having traveled more than ten miles from home, he knew he shouldn't trust his sense of direction. There *might* be a road at the far end of this meadow, or there might not. Almost certainly there was one behind him, and surely a road was a reasonable landmark to make for.

And yet...

He closed his eyes and turned, slowly, and listened to the beating of his heart. He remembered Elswyth tracing her finger over his heart, setting her spell on him, saying, "Seven days, and you will have to come to me." And when he had questioned her, she'd said he'd be drawn to her irresistibly. "You will," she'd said, "be unable to *keep* from finding me." Only one day had passed, and the tug was so faint he hadn't felt it; but he'd followed it when his mind had been too occupied to keep track of his feet. He opened his eyes and found that he was once more facing the direction he'd been unwittingly heading.

There was too much danger in the uneven ground to walk with his eyes closed, but Selwyn tried to rid his mind of any thoughts, and he began walking.

Farold roused himself at dusk.

Selwyn had indeed found the road beyond the meadow, but shortly thereafter he'd felt himself inclined to leave again. Now he was walking on what was little more than a path through the woods.

"I hate to be the one to have to tell you," Farold said in his usual accusing voice, "but are you aware that we appear to have accidentally wandered slightly out of Penryth?"

"Yes," Selwyn said.

"We are, in fact," Farold pointed out, "in a forest."

"Yes," Selwyn said.

"Is this because you've narrowed down the list of suspects to knife-wielding bears or miller's-assistant-hating wolves?"

"I'm looking for Elswyth," Selwyn muttered, expecting an outburst.

Instead, Farold practically purred, "Well, and who could blame you for missing her—sweet, lovely young thing that she is."

"Oh, shut up," Selwyn said.

He kept walking until long after dark, and Farold kept shut up for very little of that time.

Selwyn's only relief was when periodically Farold would dart away after some flying insect. But he always returned.

Still, it was Farold, with his superior bat ability to find things in the dark, who finally said, "Houses up ahead."

Selwyn stopped, and Farold veered off sharply to keep from smacking into the back of his head.

"Oh, this makes sense," Farold complained. "Hike for mile after mile of wilderness, then stop at the first sight of civilization."

"Shhh," Selwyn said. He could just barely make out the dark shapes of a cluster of houses, but not a one of them had a light showing, not this late at night. There were fewer houses than in Penryth. That and the way the tiny village was practically carved out of the woods made him think he might be in Woldham. He had never been to Woldham before, but he'd heard about it, and about the witch who lived there. So that *was* Elswyth, even though the stories he'd heard had made him think the witch of Woldham was shriveled and hunchbacked. And she only had one good eye, he re-membered. The stories definitely said the witch of Woldham had only one good eye. But perhaps, being a witch, she had found a cure. Or perhaps, being Elswyth, she had just pretended to be blind in one eye, for some reason clear only to Elswyth.

"Which house is hers?" Farold hissed, lowering his voice, but not by much.

"How should I know?" Selwyn snapped.

Farold swept off ahead of him and fluttered about the nearest house, trying to peek in through cracks in the shutter.

"Farold," Selwyn called, not daring to raise his voice. "Farold, get back here." All he needed was to wake someone, to be run out of this village, too. Somehow, he had the feeling Elswyth would not speak up to defend him.

Farold, naturally, ignored him.

But standing there in the dark, listening to hear if Farold's little bat wings made any sound, Selwyn felt a slight tug to the left. *Elswyth,* he thought. He headed in that direction, and in a moment Farold was once more by his side.

"Are you guessing, or do you know?" Farold asked.

"Shhh," Selwyn told him again.

"But—," Farold started, for Selwyn was walking beyond the small group of houses, heading for a path that led once again into the woods.

"Do you want to upset the village folk?" Selwyn asked. "Do you want to upset Elswyth?"

That quieted him.

Selwyn obeyed the sensation that drew him to a path he hadn't even seen. The path wound among several trees, then led up to a lone house surrounded by a stone wall that stood shoulder high. But he wasn't drawn to follow the path up to the gate, though he felt Elswyth was very close; he was drawn to circle to the side. Then he was drawn to climb the wall.

"You did," Farold asked, his voice uncannily loud right by Selwyn's ear, "notice the clear path and the gate with the simple latch? I wouldn't even bring it up except—"

"Shhh!" Selwyn hissed, ready to strangle him. "Would you *please* stop making so much noise?" He swung himself over the wall. And put his foot down in a wheelbarrow that was on the other side. The wheelbarrow tipped under his weight, dumping him and a load of clay pots onto a makeshift fence of sticks and twine. This fragile fence collapsed under him, landing him on top of a prickly raspberry bush. He rolled to get out of the bush, and rolled onto another. "Ouch, ouch, ouch," he gasped, unable to stifle entirely his outcries of pain. He kept rolling, and took down more of the little fence. There must have been pie tins strung up on the other side to keep the sheep away, for there was a dreadful metallic clatter as they came down. Selwyn knew it was sheep the gardener was trying to keep out, because a cluster of them immediately gathered and began to bleat *"Meee-eee-eee-eee"* at him and tried to get at the raspberry bushes.

Farold whispered into his ear, "Oh, all right, if you say so, I'll try to be more quiet."

"Shhh," Selwyn told him. "Shhh," Selwyn told the sheep.

The door to the house was flung open, throwing out

into the night a glow that Selwyn recognized as witch light. A cranky voice yelled, "You damn young hooligans! How many times do I have to tell you to keep out of my garden?"

But at the same time, a hand whacked him hard on the back of the head: Elswyth, right beside him, and not the woman who was yelling at him from the doorway after all. "Quiet!" Elswyth commanded him in an intense whisper. "You sound like a hysterical snake."

The figure in the doorway—all Selwyn could make out was her silhouette—raised her arms. A broom came flying out of the doorway, untouched by the woman's hands, over the stoop, over the yard, over the sheep, straight at where they crouched among the ruins of the raspberry fence.

"Good-bye," Farold said, flitting off into the night.

Elswyth made a gesture, and the broom ignored her and went straight for Selwyn. Though the witch in the doorway stood with her hands on her hips, the broom began beating at Selwyn's head and shoulders just as though she was standing right there, holding on to the handle.

"Ouch, ouch, ouch, ouch!" Selwyn ducked and covered his head.

Elswyth abandoned him, too, scrambling up and over the fence at a speed amazing for a woman her age. She popped back up from the other side and hissed at him: "Stupid fool! You going to stay there and let it beat you senseless?"

"Too late!" Farold called.

Selwyn had hoped that if he didn't fight back, the

broom would leave him alone, but apparently that was not to be. He climbed back over the wall—difficult as that was with the broom beating him all the while. But as soon as he dropped over onto the other side, the ill-tempered broom let him be and returned to the witch in the doorway.

"Hooligans!" she shouted again, and slammed the door shut.

But still Selwyn was not safe.

Elswyth smacked his head yet again. "Fool!" she said. "What did you think you were doing?"

"I was looking for you," Selwyn said.

"And I," Elswyth said, "was looking for one of the ingredients I need for one of my spells: milk stolen at midnight from the she sheep of a witch, and you ruined that for me."

"Sorry," Selwyn said. "You could try again later."

She smacked him again. "How many times a night does midnight come to your village?" she demanded.

He hadn't meant later that night; he'd just meant to point out he hadn't ruined the spell permanently for her.

"Fool," she repeated yet again. "Why did you want to see me? Are you ready to start your seven years of service? Have you proven who murdered the bat?"

"Not exactly," Selwyn admitted.

Farold snorted. "He's narrowed down the list of suspects," he said. "He now knows it wasn't him or me."

"What *do* you want?" Elswyth asked.

Selwyn guessed that now was probably not the best time to be asking for favors, but he couldn't wait. He said, "People were suspicious of me as a pilgrim because they didn't know me, and they were wondering why I was asking so many questions."

Elswyth smiled.

Selwyn knew he was in trouble.

THIRTEEN

"So," said Elswyth, "are you asking for a new disguise, or for a new plan entirely?"

"Some suggestions might be helpful," Selwyn said hopefully.

He should have known better.

She said, "Advice costs the same price as a disguise: one year's service. But if I have to stand here and listen to your whole boring life story so that I can figure out your best course of action, that's six additional months for every time I yawn."

Knowing how patient she could be, Selwyn hurriedly said, "A new disguise, please."

"Rich merchant and his dog," Farold whispered in

such a tiny voice he was probably trying to sound like the voice of Selwyn's own mind.

Ignoring him, Selwyn explained to Elswyth, "The problem is that the villagers aren't used to strangers. So I thought I might do better disguised as someone they know. Can you do that? Can you make me look exactly like a particular person?"

"If your description is good enough," Elswyth assured him. "We'll get a bucket of water so you can see your reflection and you and the bat can guide me as I make the changes. Of course, that takes more time, so I'll have to charge you two years."

Why wasn't that a surprise?

"Well, that's brilliant," Farold said. "Two years to disguise you as a particular person, and how many to make sure that you and that particular person don't both walk into the same particular room at the same particular time?"

"I was thinking," Selwyn explained, "it would have to be someone who doesn't live in Penryth anymore."

"Like you and me," Farold said.

"Like Alden." Alden was his neighbor Thorne's eldest son, a few years older than Selwyn and Farold, and gone with the passing of last year, when he'd left to seek a more exciting life than that of a farmer.

"Alden?" Farold said, giving a little bat hoot, *"Alden Thorneson?"*—even though there was only one Alden in the village. "What makes you think anybody would talk to him? I don't think even Thorne would be happy to see him back, good-for-nothing bully that he is. No-

body likes him. Even more than nobody likes you. Why, I could tell you stories—"

Elswyth groaned—loudly. "I'm sure you could," she said. "But I'd have to charge *you* six months for every yawn, too." She gave a great yawn, then smiled sweetly and said, very demurely, "Excuse me." Turning to Selwyn, she asked, "So, is this Alden Thorneson your choice, or just a passing thought?"

Selwyn hesitated as Farold shook his head frantically. He probably shouldn't go around looking like someone about whom he didn't know important things. "What kind of stories could you tell?" he asked Farold. "Tell me one thing, the worst."

Farold concentrated for a moment. "All right. He burned down Holt's smithy."

"That fire was caused by a lightning strike during a storm," Selwyn said.

Farold just looked at him.

"Wasn't it?" Selwyn asked.

Elswyth said, "Just because a fire starts during a storm doesn't mean the storm caused the fire."

"Exactly," Farold said. "The old biddy makes sense." He wrinkled his large bat nose, obviously begrudging even this praise, and added, "Sometimes."

Elswyth bared her teeth at him.

"Still…," Selwyn said, unwilling to believe that anybody could be that destructive. Holt had lost everything in that fire. "What makes you say Alden started it?"

"The two of them never got along. Alden liked to think up ways to torment Holt, like the time he poured grease on the firewood Holt kept out back, so that when Holt went to use the wood, the fire smoked and stank, and it was near impossible to tell which pieces had grease on them and which didn't, so Holt ended up having to cart the whole load away and chop new. Holt was always complaining to Thorne about one bit of nuisance or another that Alden was causing, and the more Holt complained, the more Alden plagued him."

Selwyn was about to say that this was little more than the kind of thing that had gotten *him* accused of killing Farold, when Farold continued, "But the night of the fire, I was coming home late from the tavern, dodging from one doorway to another trying to keep at least a bit out of the rain. I saw Alden coming out of the smithy, with no light on behind him to indicate it was late business he was up to. It never occurred to me he was doing worse than bending horseshoe nails, but he must have put a hot ember someplace where it smoldered halfway through the night, till just about the time the thunder and lightning started. And then..." Farold waved his wings, indicating the blacksmith's shop going up in flames.

"It might have been more of the usual baiting he was up to," Selwyn pointed out. "And just coincidence about the timing."

"Except," Farold said, "then why was it—when I confronted him—he was willing to pay me not to tell anybody I'd seen him?"

Elswyth gave a hoot of laughter. "You blackmailed him? The obnoxious little bat is a blackmailing bat?"

"No," Farold said. He readjusted his wings. "I just…accepted money from him…not to tell anybody what I'd seen."

"No wonder he left town," Elswyth said. "To get away from making payments to you."

Selwyn didn't find this nearly as funny as Elswyth did. "You knew he started that fire, and you didn't tell anyone?"

"What good would it have done?" Farold said. "By then the smithy was already destroyed. It wasn't as though I could have prevented it."

"But you knew it wasn't the act of God everyone supposed it was," Selwyn said.

Farold shrugged. "I loaned Holt the money to get started again."

Elswyth said, "No doubt from the money this Alden Thorneson paid you."

"Yes," Farold said, as though he didn't find anything wrong with this.

A new thought came to Selwyn. "And what of Thorne, did he know?"

"About the fire or about the money?" Farold asked, sulky because of Selwyn's accusing tone.

"Both," Selwyn said.

"Yes," Farold admitted.

"So Thorne could have wanted you dead—to protect his family's reputation, to prevent you from asking for more money."

"No," Farold said. He thought about it. "Well, maybe."

"Another suspect," Elswyth said. "I'm so pleased for you."

Selwyn knew better than to take her at her word. "Well," he said, "all things considered, I don't think I want to be disguised as Alden. But who else is there? Nobody else has left Penryth in the last ten years."

Farold thought for a moment. "That's not true," he said. "Kendra left."

"She's a girl," Selwyn objected.

"She's Orik's daughter," Farold said.

Selwyn couldn't see the point of that comment. "Which would make her a girl," he pointed out.

"Which would make her a tavern girl," Farold said. "People are always telling their problems to tavern keepers and tavern girls. What better person to be, if you want people to open up and tell you things?"

"She's a girl," Selwyn repeated, getting louder.

"You said that already," Farold told him. "She's a girl people like to talk to."

"That's why her mother sent her to the convent at Saint Hilda's," Selwyn said, "so the nuns would teach her not to listen to everything people said to her."

Farold shrugged. "Just think about it," he advised. "Alden Thorneson comes swaggering back into town from being a robber baron or pirate king or whatever other life he's made for himself, and Kendra comes back to work at her father's tavern. And they both ask, 'So, what's new?' Who are you going to talk to?"

Selwyn squirmed, knowing Farold was right. "What if Kendra comes back while I'm impersonating her?"

"Her parents sent her to be educated by the nuns,"

Farold said. "You think they could educate her in six months? She's no more likely to come back than Alden is."

Elswyth said, "It *can* be done, in case you were wondering. With the right instructions, I could make you look like a girl."

"I don't know...," Selwyn said.

Farold and Elswyth both sighed.

"Well, then, who?" Elswyth demanded.

There was no one else. Which Elswyth could no doubt see from his face. She grinned wickedly. "Last chance to pee standing up," she warned.

FOURTEEN

Elswyth made Selwyn climb back over the wall into the garden to fetch one of the clay pots he'd accidentally dumped when he tipped the wheelbarrow. He was certain that the witch of Woldham would be watching and would once more send her broom after him, but the night was silent and he even successfully hoisted the bucket up from her well to fill the pot.

"The pot isn't dark enough to reflect," Selwyn said once he'd brought it back to Elswyth.

"I can magically enhance it," Elswyth answered.

"Well then, why didn't you just magically provide the water?" Selwyn asked. "And the pot, too, for that matter?"

She smacked him on the back of the head and didn't bother to tell him why.

She got a small fire going, and something brewing on it. "Tell me about this Kendra," she said then. "What does she look like?"

"She's very pretty," Farold said.

"How did I guess you'd say that?" Elswyth muttered. "Try to be more specific. How old is she and how tall? What color hair and eyes? Is she fat or thin?"

"She's a bit older than Farold and me—," Selwyn started.

"She's eighteen years old," Farold interrupted.

"Light brown hair," Selwyn said.

"Dark blond," Farold corrected.

"Curly but not too curly," Selwyn continued.

"Down to about here." Farold fluttered halfway between Elswyth's shoulder and her elbow.

The image of Selwyn's reflection shifted as Elswyth dipped her hands into the smoke that rose from her simmering pot. Selwyn tried to concentrate only on the image and not on his own changing form. His body tingled and pulled and contracted. It had been much less disconcerting last time, to have the changes wrought while he was under the water of the stream, and to just step out and find the deed done. For the first time he realized that Elswyth had done him a kindness then—his near-drowning notwithstanding.

What am I doing? he asked himself as his features shifted, sure that this was his biggest mistake so far.

Farold was either very observant or quite good at

making up details. For the most part, Selwyn let him have his way when he insisted on the exact texture of Kendra's hair and how she parted it just slightly to the left of middle and that she had a slight—though becoming—bump on her nose and that her fingers were long and slender. But finally Selwyn put his foot down. He put it down when Farold said, "And she's got bigger...," and held his wings out in front of his chest.

"Now see here," Selwyn said as Elswyth made the correction. "Put those back to the size they were before."

She made his bosom smaller.

"He needs more," Farold assured her.

"No, I don't." Selwyn folded his arms in front of himself, partly for protection, partly to hold himself in. "Maybe smaller, even."

Farold snorted. "Bigger," he insisted.

"Smaller," Selwyn countered.

Elswyth sighed. "This is taking forever. Last change or I charge you an additional six months. Look over at the reflection, not down at yourself. Now, bigger or smaller?"

"People will notice," Farold warned. "They'll wonder, What did those nuns at Saint Hilda's *do* to Kendra?"

Selwyn looked at his reflection in the water of the clay pot. Somewhere along the way Elswyth had changed his pilgrim's robes to a dress, and now he tried to pull the bodice up higher to cover more. He closed his eyes and pictured Kendra the last time he had seen her, which had been early spring. Selwyn remembered her sitting in the back of Orik's wagon, wearing a light spring dress, blowing kisses at the young men gathered to see her off to the convent of Saint Hilda's. There had been a lot of young men, for Kendra was very well liked. He squinted through his eyelashes at the reflection and tried to think of the image as Kendra, not himself. Reluctantly, he muttered, "Slightly bigger," and closed his eyes again quickly before Elswyth could do it.

"There," she said. "And here's some free advice: Try not to trip over your skirt, and try to remember not to walk like you're stepping over the furrows in your father's field."

"All right," Selwyn muttered.

"Hey!" Farold said. "He still has his own voice."

"That's because I *disguised* him," Elswyth explained testily. "I didn't change his inner essence."

"And please don't," Selwyn said. It was bad enough to *look* like a girl.

Elswyth said, "If I did, it would cost you another three years."

"I'm sure I can manage," Selwyn said.

"Oh, I'm sure you can, too," Elswyth agreed, but she was laughing.

"What about me?" Farold said. "Aren't you worried about people in the village recognizing me as the pilgrim's French killer bat?"

Selwyn was tempted to tell him not to come back to the village—that he was more trouble than he was worth. But he remembered how Farold had been the one to tell him about Merton and the knife, and about how Thorne had known Farold was blackmailing his son. That was two more people who might have killed Farold whom Selwyn would never have known to suspect. Farold *might* come up with more important information. And he was right: People would be surprised enough to have Kendra turn up—suddenly and without notice. She definitely shouldn't have a bat as a companion.

"Six months to turn him into a dog?" Selwyn asked Elswyth.

She held her hands apart to show a size not quite the width of a hand. "A tiny dog."

Selwyn scratched behind his ear, a habit he had when thinking, and was momentarily disconcerted by all the hair he found on his head. A dog that tiny was sure to get stepped on. And it might be convenient to have Farold know how to fly. "Maybe a little songbird?" he suggested. "In a cage? That's something Kendra might bring home as a remembrance from the nuns."

"Cage?" Farold squawked.

"For your own safety," Selwyn assured him.

"Six months," Elswyth said. "Gather some sticks for me to make the cage."

FIFTEEN

After a night's rest in the woods, Selwyn and Farold once again parted company with Elswyth and set off for Penryth: Selwyn—a young man disguised as a young woman—who had to concentrate on every step so as not to trip over his long skirt; and Farold—a dead man in the body of a bat disguised as a goldfinch— who was working very hard to get a goldfinch's song out from between what were in reality bat lips.

"Less whistle," Selwyn advised, "more twitter."

"Drop dead," Farold grumbled, without a trace of birdsong in his voice. He clung to the side of the cage, ignoring the hanging swing Elswyth had made, which she had insisted a bird would love. He added, "You're making me seasick, swinging this cage back and forth, and back and forth"—Selwyn stepped on the edge of his skirt and stumbled and Farold continued—"and up and down—"

"And over the hedge and down the hill," Selwyn threatened.

"At this point, it would only be a kindness," Farold moaned.

"Shhh," Selwyn said.

"Pardon me for not suffering quietly enough to suit you," Farold said.

"Shhh," Selwyn repeated more urgently. "Someone's coming."

From the direction they were heading came the rumbling of cart wheels. Selwyn looked up from his feet and the dirt road, taking note of his surroundings for the first time in a long while: He was closer to the village than he had realized. This would be the fields of Raedan and his brother Merton that he was passing.

His first inclination was to dive into the bushes that lined the road, to postpone meeting anyone, though the whole purpose of being disguised and returning to Penryth was to be among people. Besides, what if whoever was coming had heard him talking? And that was a double-edged question, for what if whoever was coming had recognized his voice, or Farold's?

There was hardly time to begin to think of all the possibilities of what could go wrong, no time at all to worry or to decide what he *should* do. Raedan came walking around the curve of the road, pulling behind him the two-wheeled cart with which he would have brought produce to market, now piled high with wool his mother and sisters would spend the winter spinning and weaving.

Seeing Selwyn, Raedan stopped so suddenly, the cart bumped him from behind.

He'll never believe for a moment, Selwyn thought. What had he gotten himself into?

"Kendra!" Raedan exclaimed in delight. Dropping the handles of the cart, he ran forward and—before Selwyn could stop him—had swept Selwyn up. Whether Selwyn still weighed what he would as a man, or whether he was made ungainly because he was unused to people picking him up and swinging him around, he and Raedan and the skirt and the birdcage all got entangled and they came close to ending up in a heap on the road.

Raedan was too elated to notice—or at least to comment. "Kendra, it's wonderful to see you again!"

Selwyn locked his elbows to keep Raedan from pulling him in any closer, putting Farold's cage, as well as Raedan, at arm's length. Raedan was his closest friend, but he wasn't *that* close.

Farold clung to the bars of his swaying cage, wearing the expression of a storm-tossed sailor.

Selwyn cleared his throat twice, hesitating, but he had to speak eventually. In a husky whisper, he said, "I'm happy to see you, too, Raedan." To excuse the voice, and to forestall any inclination Raedan might have for any warmer welcome, he quickly added, "Pardon my slight indisposition." He gave a loud sniff. "I've had a cold for days."

"You're still the most beautiful girl in Penryth," Raedan said.

Do I look that lovesick and silly when I'm talking to Anora? Selwyn wondered. *Do I tell her such foolish-sounding things?* "Thank you," he murmured, ducking his head and hiding his face modestly with the edge of the shawl Elswyth had made for him from two of her squares of wool. He didn't point out that Anora was more beautiful. "You're so kind. How are my parents?"

"Fine," Raedan said. "They'll be overjoyed to see you."

"I hope so." Selwyn's voice broke into a shaky falsetto. He held the shawl up over his mouth and coughed delicately. "I can hardly wait to see them." He started moving in the direction of the village, which he thought meant an end to the conversation, but Raedan, who'd been returning from there and was little more than a stone's throw from home, picked up the handles of the cart, pivoted it around, and began walking by Selwyn's side.

"Here, let me," Raedan said, taking the birdcage from Selwyn's grasp. "A special treat for your homecoming supper?"

"A remembrance from the nuns of Saint Hilda's," Selwyn explained, enjoying Farold's panicked peeps and feather rustlings. Raedan balanced the cage—precariously, Selwyn thought—on the mound of wool. He hoped Farold wouldn't forget himself and start making fun, or complaining, or vomiting from the motion. *Did* finches wrap their wings around their stomachs when they felt ill?

Raedan gave Selwyn's shoulders a squeeze. "You're just what this old village needs," he said wholeheartedly. "Terrible things have happened."

"Oh?" Selwyn said. "Anything that I should know about?"

Raedan hesitated.

"Even if it's bad news"—Selwyn was aware that his voice was going up, down, and around, and he wished he'd practiced talking as well as walking—"even if it's bad news, somebody has to tell me eventually."

Raedan took a deep breath. "It *is* bad news," he said, "though nothing touching your family directly. It's Farold, the miller's nephew...He's dead."

Selwyn was peeved that Raedan mentioned Farold first. Still, it was a logical place to start, rather than with the condemned murderer. "The poor dear," he said. "A drinking accident?"

"No accident at all. He was murdered."

"Really?" Selwyn tried to sound shocked. "Who would do such a thing? Was it Linton?"

Farold gave a very unfinchlike snort.

"No," Raedan said slowly. "Why would you ask that?"

"It just seemed to stand to reason. Who *was* accused?"

"Selwyn," Raedan answered. "Selwyn Roweson."

"No," Selwyn said. "Not that nice boy."

"Mind, I'm not saying he did it." Luckily, Raedan was watching Selwyn and didn't see Farold, behind him in the cart, making frantic hushing motions at Selwyn. How did Farold ever expect him to get information about the murder without talking about it? Selwyn returned his attention to Raedan, who was saying, "But, unfortunately, all the circumstances seemed to point to him."

"What…"—Selwyn remembered his voice and started again more quietly—"what circumstances?"

"Well, for one thing, there was long-standing rivalry between the two of them over Bowden's daughter, Anora, which ended with Anora agreeing to marry Farold."

Selwyn made a dismissive sound. "A bad choice, there. But, anyway, that's nothing definite. Most likely she would have come to her senses eventually and changed her mind."

Farold spit on the bottom of the cage.

"Possibly," Raedan admitted. "But it was Selwyn's knife that killed Farold."

"Anyone," Selwyn said darkly, "can find someone's knife and use it."

"Again, possibly," Raedan said so smoothly Selwyn couldn't tell whether he knew about his brother's having found the knife or not. "But first Selwyn swore he had never been in the village that night, and then—when he found out there was a witness—he admitted he had. It's hard to believe someone whose story keeps changing."

Fool, fool, and fool! Selwyn chided himself for that useless and damning lie. "Maybe he was afraid," he said.

"Who wouldn't be?" Raedan agreed sympathetically.

"Who was the witness?" Selwyn asked.

"Your mother."

It took him a moment to realize that Raedan meant Kendra's mother, Wilona, and not his own. He couldn't, in any case, start poking at her credibility.

"I didn't think he did it," Raedan said. "It's not like him."

"No," Selwyn agreed breathlessly.

"But he was executed for it."

Selwyn couldn't bring himself to ask how, though surely Kendra would have wondered. Raedan had spoken as though it was past; and Selwyn realized with a sick feeling that there was no reason anyone would believe he could have survived in the burial cave this long. Without Elswyth's intervention, he *would* have been dead by now. In another day or two, once everyone was convinced Selwyn must be dead, they would be releasing his father. *And then what?* he thought.

By that time they were almost into Penryth, and one voice then another called, "Ho, Kendra!" People came running out to greet him. He had to force himself to be jovial, for Kendra had no special reason to grieve for Selwyn Roweson, no matter how grim his fate.

Girls hugged him and kissed him on the cheek, which was a delicious—though frustrating—sensation. He did his best to avoid the men who would do the same. Several times he was pinched or patted on the bottom. It was not that Selwyn had forgotten how well liked Kendra was, it was just that he had not realized how much enthusiasm people would show.

Then, finally, bringing a crowd with him, he was at the tavern. Orik and Wilona stood in the doorway, both with arms open. Selwyn chose to go to Orik first so that he would have an excuse to break away almost instantly to hug his "mother."

"Father," he murmured, giving a little cough and sniff. "Mother." He gave a sniff and cough. "Please excuse my cold." He forced a sneeze.

Orik was beaming; Wilona was weeping with joy.

"Come in, everyone," Orik invited. "Help us celebrate."

People cheered, apparently willing to go into the tavern—and put up with having to see Selwyn's father tied up in the corner—if free drinks were involved.

Farold squawked loudly, a reminder—in case Selwyn needed one—that he was there, and not to be left out in the street in Raedan's cart. He sounded more like a chicken than a finch; but Selwyn gave Kendra's brightest smile and brought the cage in with him.

Inside, Wilona took hold of his arm, apparently reluctant to let go, which Selwyn would have excused as motherly excitement at a daughter's return, but Wilona kept dragging on the arm, tugging him in the direction of the back of the tavern, to the family's living quarters.

Oh no! Selwyn thought. The last thing he wanted was to be alone with the mother of the woman he was disguised as.

"Orik," Wilona called over the heads of the crowd of well-wishers who were gathering in the room.

She caught her husband's eye. "One free round," Orik announced to the crowd. Then, "Linton." He held up a forefinger. "You're in charge."

This was not like him at all, to leave customers in the care of customers.

Selwyn realized he'd been wrong before: The last thing he wanted was to be with both the mother *and* the father of the woman he was disguised as.

The three of them made their way from the tavern into the living quarters, and Orik closed the adjoining door behind them, which only cut down a bit on the noise.

Orik leaned against the door and Wilona folded her arms across her chest and looked at Selwyn.

Selwyn gulped, knowing for sure that something was wrong.

Wilona asked, "What happened with the baby?"

In the cage, Farold made a noise that sounded very much like "Oops."

SIXTEEN

"Baby," Selwyn echoed, trying to sound as though he was simply repeating, not questioning—and at the same time trying desperately to think what Orik and Wilona could possibly mean, beyond, of course, the obvious: that Kendra had been sent to the convent at Saint Hilda's not solely for the purpose of education, but to hide the fact that she—an unmarried young woman—was with child.

"The baby," Wilona said, impatience tingeing her voice. "You don't need to be coy with us. *We* knew about your condition; *we're* the ones who made the arrangements with the nuns."

"Of course," Selwyn said, still stalling for time. He glanced into the birdcage he still held, on the chance that Farold might be able to give him some guidance. Farold shrugged his fat little yellow shoulders.

Selwyn saw that Wilona looked ready to shake him. He licked his lips. Hesitantly he said, "*Ahm*, the nuns agreed to raise it."

"*It?*" Wilona demanded shrilly. "Are we talking about a puppy here, or your child?"

Selwyn had to plunge in. The real Kendra had certainly not been showing her pregnancy when she left Penryth in April, which had to mean she'd only just recently had her baby—*if* she'd even really had it yet. Trusting that she hadn't found a way to inform her parents, he took a guess. "The nuns agreed to raise her," he said, mumbling the last word, so that if Orik and Wilona said, "We thought you sent word you'd had a boy," he could tell them that he had, that he'd just now said *him* and they must have misheard.

But obviously Kendra *hadn't* sent word. Wilona clasped her hands. "A girl," she cried. "A sweet little baby girl."

Selwyn despised himself for playing with this family's lives this way.

Orik grumbled, "Just so long as the nuns are willing to keep her on, and your shame doesn't spread to your mother and me and your little brothers."

Kendra's brothers were five years old, and seven, and eight. Selwyn couldn't see how anything Kendra did would reflect on them.

Apparently Wilona couldn't, either. She gave her husband a poke. "We've been through all that already," she said. "Now is the time to be happy that it's all over, and the child is provided for, and Kendra is back with us." She gave Selwyn a fierce hug.

"Well, now that you're back," Orik said, "you can help serve drinks."

"Yes, Father," Selwyn said meekly.

Orik put his hand on the door, but then he turned back. "Oh," he said as though trying to sound matter-of-fact. "You'll be hearing it soon anyway, so you'd best hear it from me now."

"What, Father?"

"Young Selwyn Roweson went and killed Farold."

He sounded downright joyful, which left Selwyn at a loss for words.

"Now, now, dear," Wilona said, patting Selwyn's hand. "It's all for the best, I'm sure. You agreed it was all a mistake with Farold and you never really loved him."

Selwyn was getting an awful feeling he might know what they were talking about.

Orik said, "*I* look at it as Selwyn doing us a favor. *I* look at it as one less worm in the world to lead inno-cent young girls astray."

"Farold?" Selwyn said, his voice a whispered croak, never mind trying to sound like a girl. He remembered Farold telling how he'd happened upon Alden Thorne-son the night of the fire in the smithy. "I was coming home late from the tavern," Farold had said. Every-thing fell into place. He didn't dare lift up the birdcage. One look at Farold's face—any of Farold's faces— would be enough to make him lose control, he knew.

He would have to open the cage and wring that little goldfinch neck.

"Could I...," Selwyn started. "Would you mind... That is..."

"I think poor Kendra needs a moment to herself," Wilona told Orik. "It has to be a shock, no matter what."

"I suppose," Orik agreed grumpily. "But not too long. I'll need you out there once the crowd starts buying."

"Yes, Father," Selwyn managed to say.

As soon as the door shut behind Kendra's parents, Selwyn lifted the cage to eye level.

Farold was shaking his head. If Selwyn believed bats disguised as goldfinches could go pale, he'd say Farold paled.

"You," Selwyn said.

"No," Farold said.

"How could you let me disguise myself—"

"No," Farold repeated.

"—as a girl?"

"Selwyn, listen to me."

"You *suggested,* and all the while you knew—"

"I *didn't* know."

"You *should* have known—"

"I *couldn't* have known." Farold was jumping up and down in the cage. Luckily the crowd in the tavern beyond the door was noisy, because the two of them had gotten louder and louder, and now Farold shouted, "Selwyn, you dumb twit, would you listen to me?"

"I've listened to you enough."

"It wasn't me."

Selwyn shook the cage.

"It wasn't me," Farold screamed. "I didn't know she was sent away to have a baby, because it isn't my baby."

"It sounds to me," Selwyn shouted back at him, shaking the cage even harder, "as though Kendra told her parents it was. *She* should know."

"So should I," Farold said. He said it so quietly but decisively that Selwyn stopped shaking the cage. "It wasn't me," Farold said yet again.

Selwyn thought about this. "Are you certain?" he asked.

"Absolutely. Selwyn, I swear to you, I'm innocent."

Under the circumstances, how could Selwyn possibly refuse to believe that? He sighed and tried to fit the situation to a different explanation. "I suppose," he said, "Kendra could have lied to her parents to protect the real father of her child."

" 'Protect,' " Farold echoed hollowly.

"Orik told her"—Selwyn began, then corrected—"told me...that I..."—he got flustered again—"that Selwyn killed him...I mean you."

Farold said, "Maybe he was afraid, or just didn't want to admit to his daughter that he was the one who killed me."

"Or it could be," Selwyn said, "simply that he is relieved that someone else did it and saved him the trouble: He isn't necessarily the one."

Farold's feathers drooped, and Selwyn wished he could take back those words.

"Maybe we better go back into the tavern and start talking with people," Selwyn suggested. "See what we can find out."

"Sure, why not?" Farold said dejectedly. "See who else wanted me dead."

SEVENTEEN

It didn't take long for Selwyn to decide he wasn't cut out for the life of a tavern girl. If one more man looked down his dress or touched his bottom, he was going to have to start knocking heads.

His father was still tied in the chair in the corner of the tavern, though the room was so crowded Selwyn knew there would be no chance to talk without being overheard. Even so, he filled a cup with ale and brought it to him.

His father looked at him stonily. His hands, of course, were tied behind his back.

"If you would like," Selwyn said in his best attempt at a girl's voice, not daring to give any kind of signal to his father with so many others around, "I could hold the cup for you while you drink."

His father shook his head.

Selwyn said earnestly, "I would like to talk to you about Selwyn." It was the closest he could come to saying anything of substance now, even knowing that his father—as everyone else—would take it as Kendra offering a dead man's father her condolences.

His father closed his eyes and said nothing.

Someone passing by snatched the cup out of Selwyn's hand and breezily said, "Thank you, dearie." There was no more excuse to be standing there, and Selwyn went to fetch more drinks to pass around.

On the way back, Derian Miller, Farold's uncle, put his arm over Selwyn's shoulders. "A sad business," he said, nodding his head back toward Selwyn's father.

"Yes," Selwyn said. He moved to slip away, but he couldn't—stuck as he was in the space where the tavern counter met the wall—not without being obvious about it, which Kendra had never seemed to be, no matter how drunk or persistent Orik's customers became.

"Sad for all of us," the miller said. He was old and distracted and had—Selwyn remembered only after Derian had said it—as much right to be sad as Selwyn's father. More right, even, in people's view: For, though each had lost a boy he'd raised, everyone believed Selwyn's father had raised a murderer. Derian's eyes were wet and his hand on Selwyn's shoulder shook.

Selwyn flinched but managed to say calmly, "Still,

it's cruel on Rowe." His father's name felt strange in his mouth. Nervously, he went to cross his arms over his chest but found his usual placement not readily accessible. That left choosing between resting his arms very loosely over his abdomen, which made him look as though he had a stomach pain, or folding them high up on top of his bosom, which just looked silly. He let his arms drop limply down by his sides.

"You have a good heart, to worry about such things," Derian was telling him. "But he isn't left tied up like that all day. Thorne or Bowden or one of the others releases him several times a day; they let him eat, exercise, relieve himself. At night he sleeps at Holt's, tied to the anvil. It's just nobody dares leave him unwatched. He's always been a hasty man. Hasty men do hasty things."

Selwyn was relieved to hear that all was not as bad as it could have been. He asked, "What about"—he remembered in time not to say *my*—"the mother and grandmother?"

"What?" Derian asked, indicating to speak directly into his ear, and he moved in even closer.

Selwyn repeated, "What about the mother and grandmother?"

Derian gave his shoulder another squeeze. "What a kind girl you are, Kendra! Watched, though not as closely. It's been explained to each of them: Try to rescue Selwyn, and the other two members of the family will pay. But Rowe—he's not the kind of man you take chances with. Even now, when—God willing— it's all over. They'll probably release him tomorrow."

Derian sighed. "At least they still have each other—Rowe and Nelda. I'm left with no one." Derian shook his head. "No one."

The old man was suddenly shaking with silent crying. His hand slipped down a bit from Selwyn's shoulder—purely accidental, Selwyn was sure, given Derian's age and frailty and the circumstances—but Selwyn was uncomfortable and felt close to panic. What was he to do?

Selwyn said the first thing that came into his head. "But it must have been hard for them—Selwyn and his parents—to be abandoned by their friends."

"Hard for Selwyn's parents' friends?" Derian repeated, leaning in closer yet and still mishearing. "Well"—he wiped at his face—"I did my best to help, you know, that day they determined Selwyn was the one killed my boy."

"Did you?" asked Selwyn, who had not noticed any help from Derian, and very little from anybody else.

"I saw him, in the village that night. The next day at Bowden's house, before they even brought Selwyn and Rowe in, your mother stepped right up and said *she'd* seen him walking past the tavern. So I thought to myself, 'Between that, and the fight two weeks ago, and the knife—the boy is as good as convicted. There's no call for me to take his dignity away from him, telling about him sitting under the back window of Bowden's house, weeping his eyes out.'"

"Weeping his eyes out" was an exaggeration. But Selwyn had sat down when it was apparent he couldn't get Anora's attention without risk of waking the rest of her household. And he had, he grudgingly admitted, rested his head on his knees, which might have looked like crying, though surely there had not been more than a tear or two. The miller had not shared this detail—which had nothing to do with the matter at hand—with those crowded into Bowden's room; so obviously Derian *had* seen him and wasn't just making this up to impress Kendra that he, too, had a kind heart.

Selwyn was rescued from having to say anything by Holt the blacksmith, who came up behind Derian and slapped him genially on the back, saying, "Time to share her, old man."

Derian whirled around, which gave Selwyn the room to take a step away from the wall. The miller gave a rueful smile. "Just an old man unburdening his sorrows to a sympathetic young lass," he said, wiping at his eye.

"Sorry to interrupt," Holt said, "for something so trivial as a request for a drink."

"Don't let Orik hear you call a drink trivial," Selwyn said, glad for the excuse to duck beneath the counter to fetch one. At the same time he mentally reminded himself, *FATHER, you idiot. Orik is supposed to be your father.*

If either Holt or Derian noticed the lapse, they didn't comment. Instead, Derian said, "I won't be imposing my company on you young people any longer"—even though Holt was a good dozen years older than Kendra—and he moved away while Holt leaned his elbows on the counter.

Holt frowned. "Is there something wrong with that bird you brought back with you from the convent?"

Selwyn looked where Holt was looking—where he'd set Farold's cage on one of the upturned barrels behind the counter. Farold was hanging upside down from the bar that Elswyth had provided as a swing.

Selwyn stifled a sigh for the nocturnal habits of bats. "Silly thing," he said. "Sometimes it likes to pretend it's dead."

"Ah," Holt said, as though that made sense.

Selwyn placed an overflowing cup of ale in front of him.

Holt took a long drink, then said, "It would be easier to sympathize with the man"—he inclined his head toward Derian, who was talking with other people across the room—"if his nephew hadn't been such a ..."

Selwyn raised his eyebrows, but Holt—perhaps because he thought he was talking to a lady—didn't finish.

"You didn't like Farold?" Selwyn asked. He fought an inclination to glance back at the cage, to shake Farold awake to make sure he heard.

"Well, Farold was Farold." Holt motioned for his cup to be refilled. "What else can anyone say?"

He seemed to be going to leave it at that. Selwyn said, "Odd, though, don't you think, that Selwyn would kill him?"

"I know it's a hard thing to say," Holt told him, "but it worked out well for me."

"Did it?" Selwyn asked, almost forgetting the girl's voice.

Holt nodded. "Farold loaned me money to get

started again after that fire last year. It's been a good year for me—very good—but Farold was charging"— Holt shook his head—"a *lot* of interest."

Selwyn mopped up a spill but this time couldn't refrain from looking at Farold's cage. Farold still hung from the swing, the picture of a snoring, upside-down, perfectly innocent goldfinch with nothing bothering its conscience.

"I still could have managed," Holt said, "until the marriage with Anora was settled. All of a sudden he had to have the money back right away to set up a proper household for her." He finished his second drink. "Nothing but the best would do. Of course, my debt now comes beholden to Derian, but he's willing to wait the original agreed-on two years."

Selwyn couldn't decide what Kendra would say. He couldn't decide what *he* would say. Could Holt have killed Farold to avoid having to pay back the money he owed? He remembered how Holt had been one of the few to speak up for him. Had that been because of a guilty conscience? Had it been because—of them all—Holt had *known* Selwyn wasn't guilty, regardless of the evidence?

Once Holt wandered away from the counter to talk with other people, Selwyn went to the shelf where there was a platter with a loaf of bread and some sliced mutton, in case anyone wanted food with their drink. *Blackmailing,* Selwyn thought, breaking off the end of the bread, *money mongering,*—he picked a small chunk of the hard crust—*bat.* He threw, aiming between the bars of the cage, at Farold. Too big. The bit of bread bounced off the wooden slats of the cage. He tried a smaller piece. It entered the cage, but missed Farold. The third piece hit Farold on the head.

Farold jerked awake. Hanging like a bat, but using a goldfinch's feet, he lost hold of the swing and dropped to the bottom of the cage with a squawk that sounded nothing like bat or goldfinch.

"Good shot for a girl!" called Merton, making Selwyn jump because he'd had no idea anyone was standing so close.

Stupid, he chided himself, knowing he was lucky Farold only glared and ruffled his feathers and didn't start berating him.

Annoyed at his own reckless foolishness, and still angry about the business with the knife Merton had taken then never spoken up about, and irritated at the condescension in Merton's voice, Selwyn filled Merton's cup with ale, then intentionally let go before Merton's fingers closed around it.

"Oops. Clumsy me," he said as Merton wiped ineffectually at his sodden front. Selwyn smiled, then turned around and walked away without getting Merton another.

EIGHTEEN

The crowd didn't disperse from the tavern until long after dark. After a week with no customers, Orik was so full of himself Selwyn had a hard time resisting the urge to push him facedown in a tub of ale—especially since he was, in Selwyn's estimation, the most likely suspect for having murdered Farold.

Finally Bowden and Holt announced it was time to take Selwyn's father and settle him down for the night in the smithy. Hours spent no more than a room's length away from him, and Selwyn had not had the chance to speak more than that one offer of a drink. *Tomorrow,* he thought. Somehow he would arrange a way to see him privately tomorrow. His mother, too, he made plans to talk to. When she had come to bring the prisoner his meals—escorted by Bowden's loud and bossy wife—she had looked pale and drawn, and had such dark shadows under her eyes and at her cheeks that Selwyn had had to look away. Surely, tomorrow morning, Bowden and his family could have no objection to Kendra paying her a visit.

But for tonight, finally they were all gone: his parents and their guards, the customers, the lingerers. It was time for cleaning up.

Wilona said, "I can do it myself, Kendra. You've had such a long day—walking from Saint Hilda's, catching up on all the news, fetching and serving without a break between the afternoon crowd and the evening. On your feet all day." She patted Selwyn's hand. "You need a rest."

"No," Selwyn assured her, "I'm fine. I'd prefer to stay up a bit longer."

Wilona looked ready to settle in next to him.

"*You* go to bed, Mother," he said—he hoped Kendra called her "Mother" and not some girlish pet name. "Really, you should. You've been working hard: cooking and cleaning and making things run smoothly all day."

"This is not our daughter," Orik roared, which nearly caused Selwyn to stop breathing. But then Orik gave him a swift hug and continued, "This is some hardworking girl the nuns have substituted for our Kendra."

"Oh, Orik," Wilona complained in a tone of both exasperation and love that reminded Selwyn of his own parents and nearly broke his heart.

Orik kissed Selwyn on the forehead. "Welcome back, girl," he said. "Welcome, from the bottom of my heart."

"Thank you, Father," Selwyn said awkwardly, feeling guilty now for wanting to drown Orik in his own ale. *But don't get sentimental toward him,* he reminded himself. The fact that he loved his family was not proof that he hadn't murdered Farold. It was, in fact, a good, strong motive.

As Orik headed back toward the section of the house behind the tavern, Wilona said, "Let me help you, Kendra. I insist. It will give us a chance to talk together."

A chance to talk together was not anything Selwyn looked forward to. He smiled as sweetly as he could manage and said, "I'd like that. Truly. We *do* need to talk. But not tonight, Mother. After all the noise of today"—he gestured vaguely—"my ears need a rest." That didn't come out sounding the way he wanted. "My *mind* needs a rest. And my voice." He cleared his throat to remind them of Kendra's supposed cold.

He wasn't making much sense, but Wilona said, "I know. I understand." And she also kissed him on the forehead. "If you're sure."

He nodded.

The door had no sooner closed behind her than Farold started, "Well—"

Selwyn whirled on him, with a frantic finger to his lips.

Wilona reopened the door. "Did you call after me, dear?"

"No, Mother," Selwyn said, noisily pushing one of

the benches up against the wall. "Unless you think I sound like wood scraping on the floor."

Wilona blew him a kiss and shut the door.

Selwyn held up a warning finger to Farold.

Farold sighed—several times, loudly—as Selwyn wiped down all the tables, benches, and stools, then swept the floor. Selwyn refused to talk until he had gathered up the cups and plates and brought them into the kitchen, which had the whole width of the tavern to separate him from the room where Orik and Wilona were either asleep or trying to sleep. Then he brought Farold's cage into the kitchen, too.

"Quietly now," Selwyn said as he began to clean the dishes, "what have we learned?"

Farold said, "That we probably should have had Elswyth make your bosom smaller."

Irritated, Selwyn smacked the wet rag against the side of the cage, splattering Farold with sudsy water. Then, "Shhh," he warned before Farold could sputter a complaint. "*I* learned," he said, "that it's amazing nobody killed you a long time ago."

"What?" Farold asked innocently. "Who have you been talking to? Is somebody spreading lies about me?"

"What's this about demanding back the money you loaned Holt—money you got from blackmailing Alden and his father, Thorne? Suddenly you had to have that money back after less than a year, instead of the two you promised, because you wanted it to impress Anora?"

"Oh," Farold said.

"'Oh,'" Selwyn repeated. And, when Farold didn't continue, "That's a fine defense you offer, Farold."

"I don't *need* to offer a defense," Farold said. "I'm the dead man, remember? Not the suspect."

"We're not talking about who murdered you. We're talking about you being a nasty, worthless creature."

"You know, I can leave whenever I want," Farold warned him. "People don't shout at you in the afterlife."

It was a worrisome thought, no matter what. "You get me feeling all sorry for you and concerned about your bruised feelings, then I learn that you're so thoughtless, you would demand Holt pay you back when you knew that would have ruined him."

"It wouldn't necessarily have ruined him," Farold said. Grudgingly he added, "It might have hurt a bit. But I needed the money. I couldn't very well marry Anora and ask her to move into my little room under the stairs. And we couldn't all move into Uncle Derian's room or ask him to trade rooms with us: 'Excuse me, Uncle Derian, could you move from the big room at the front of the house and up off the street, to the cubbyhole right next to the machinery?' The only way was to build on a new room, and it had to be furnished. With Uncle Derian never marrying, there hasn't been a woman living at the mill since my parents died."

"You have—had—a lot of money coming in from the mill," Selwyn pointed out. He had a sudden thought. "Didn't you? Or has the mill been in financial trouble since you took over the running of it?" *Maybe,* he thought, *DERIAN had killed Farold.* Derian, living at the mill, certainly had a better opportunity for it than Merton or Orik or Thorne or Holt, or even Linton, who had been Selwyn's first suspect. If Farold's mismanagement was causing the mill to lose money... and maybe he had refused to turn it back over to Derian ...

But Farold was shaking his head. "No," Farold said, obviously offended. "The mill made more money this year under me than any year previously."

"Well, if you had so much money, why did you need what you'd loaned Holt?"

"Because Derian is still the owner. The money from the mill is his."

Selwyn thought how his father had been willing to help clear the new field when there had been the possibility that Selwyn might marry Anora. But families were different, and if Derian hadn't been willing to advance the money to Farold, Selwyn supposed he could see how Farold would panic and turn to Holt. Though Anora, he was sure, would have understood and wouldn't have demanded luxurious accommodations. She was too sweet and kindhearted to allow harm to come to anyone on her behalf, even indirectly.

"All right," Selwyn said, "so not Derian. That leaves Orik, who thinks you're the father of his unmarried daughter's child..." He held out his thumb to begin counting.

"And Wilona, for the same reason," Farold pointed out.

Selwyn's immediate reaction was to say no, but he thought about it. The murderer had stabbed Farold in the back during the night, apparently counting on his being asleep, on his not putting up a fight. A woman, not being as strong as a man, may well have chosen this kind of a sneak attack. "Maybe," he acknowledged, and counted off his forefinger. Then he went on, "Or Holt, so he wouldn't have to pay you back the money he owed you. Or Thorne, to make sure you didn't tell people what you knew about his son. Or Alden, for blackmailing him—"

"*Alden?*" Farold hooted. "Alden is a wonderful suspect if you don't mind that he doesn't live here anymore. Come back from God-knows-where to kill me nine months after the fact, then disappear back into the night without a trace?"

"Maybe," Selwyn insisted, but he put down the finger that represented Alden. Then he put it back up as he resumed counting. "Linton, so the mill would pass down to him—"

"Always a stretch," Farold observed.

Selwyn ignored him and switched to his other hand, ending with six. "And Merton."

"Why would Merton want me dead?"

"I have no idea," Selwyn said. "But he's the one person besides you who knew about the knife."

Farold didn't argue.

"There *wasn't* anybody else who knew about the knife, was there?"

"No," Farold said.

"So why *would* Merton want you dead?" Selwyn asked.

"I already told you: I don't know."

"I thought you might have remembered something you failed to tell me before. Like with Alden and Thorne and Holt and, to a certain extent, Kendra. *Is* there?"

"No," Farold said grumpily. "You're adding more and more possibilities, but nobody for whom all the pieces fit. And you're not getting any closer to proving anything."

"I know," Selwyn grumbled. "Tomorrow we'll have to find some excuse to take a look at your room—see if we can learn anything there."

"We can try," Farold said. "But I doubt, after almost a week, that we'll find anything."

Selwyn thought he was probably right, but he only said, "In the meantime, I'm going to let you out of your cage." He unfastened the twine that held the door, which was really an enchanted bit of vine tied on pieces of sticks. "Try flying around the houses of the suspects. Maybe you'll see or overhear something."

Farold fluttered around the room to stretch his wings, then sat on top of the cage. "Oh, that's very likely," he said with exaggerated enthusiasm. "At this hour what I'm likely to see is people sleeping, and what I'll overhear is snoring."

"I'll leave the cage door open so you can get in and out," Selwyn said, ignoring his sarcasm. "Maybe you'll learn something tomorrow. Try to stay out of people's way. If anybody asks, I'll have to say you escaped. But Kendra is so well liked that everyone will try to recapture you for her. Still, make sure you check back with me regularly so that we can tell each other what we've learned."

"So what you're saying," Farold said, "is stay around people so I can watch them, but keep away lest they see me. And all the while keep coming back here, where everybody will be trying to catch me to impress you."

Selwyn smacked the cage with the wet rag again, and Farold took to the air. "Just go," Selwyn told him. "Keep out of the ale barrels." He opened the back door, then went to get the basin of wash water to dump it.

The first thing he noticed when he stepped outside was that Farold had not flown away but was perched on the open door, chirping a bad imitation of a goldfinch song. Then Selwyn saw why. Anora, too, was just emptying a basin of wash water into the alley. He had not seen her in the tavern today; he had not seen her since the day he'd been dragged out of her father's house to the burial cave.

Now, even though she had her back to him, at first he couldn't get his voice to work. This turned out to be good, because in that extra moment he remembered to disguise his voice. "Hello," he said in the throaty whisper that—if it didn't exactly sound like a girl's voice—at least didn't sound quite like a man's.

Anora whirled around, which caused a good amount of the water she was pouring out to end up on his feet and legs. Hastily she righted the basin, though there couldn't have been much water left inside. She must have been too embarrassed to respond to his greeting, for she just stood there, looking at him in the alleyway that was lit only by the candlelight spilling out from both their doorways.

His kind, beautiful Anora. The sight of her left Selwyn breathless. Suddenly everything was clear to him: Farold was a terrible helper-companion-investigator to be saddled with. Sweet Anora would be much more help in solving the crime and proving his innocence. He knew he'd have to be careful, so as not to frighten her. But he was sure, once he explained all that had happened, she would be eager to help him.

He turned so that he could dump out the water he carried without splashing her, and at the same time he started to work out what would be the best way to tell her all that he needed to tell her.

Without warning, a bucketful of cold, greasy water hit his back. Selwyn gasped in surprise and whirled to find Anora had upended her basin over him. And he'd been wrong: There *had* been a significant amount left in the bottom.

Even Farold was stunned into silence, his beak parted but his song cut off midchirp.

"What—," Selwyn started, forgetting to disguise his voice, but cold and surprise made it go high all on its own.

"How *dare* you come back?" Anora spit at him.

She knows who I am, he thought. *And she believes I'm the one who killed Farold.*

The thought that she didn't believe in his innocence

left him speechless. It was another fortunate delay, for she continued, "You slut, you harlot, you worthless piece of garbage."

"But..." Selwyn had no idea where to go to from there.

Anora swung her basin, hitting his arm. "Why didn't you just stay away, Kendra?"

Selwyn caught hold of the edge of the basin as she started to make a second swing with it. "What are you talking about?"

"'What are you talking about?'" Anora mimicked in a cruel singsong. "Don't play innocent with me. Your mother told my mother *all* about you. *I* know where you've been." She gave up trying to wrest the basin out of Selwyn's grip.

"When?" Selwyn demanded, for Wilona had spent all day helping in the tavern, and Anora's mother had only come in for the briefest moments, while escorting his real mother when she brought in meals for the prisoner. "When did our mothers talk?"

Apparently Anora guessed what Selwyn was thinking. "Not today, *stupid*," she hissed. "More than a week ago. Your mother was *so* pleased with herself, saying you might be coming back home from the convent soon. And when my mother said six months was much too soon for a girl to learn refined manners and that you were rather *old* to be sent to the nuns anyway, your mother let it slip why you had *really* gone. Well, you ruined everything, you horrid little slut. I could have been the daughter of the headman *and* the wife of the wealthiest merchant in Penryth. Everyone would have envied me. And Farold wasn't even too bad-looking. But I had to call off the betrothal because of you, and make other arrangements, which aren't nearly as much to my liking. How could I possibly marry Farold when you were carrying his bastard and that child would always be the firstborn instead of one of mine?"

Selwyn was left stunned by this sudden flood of malevolence from his gentle Anora.

"But now Farold is dead," Anora said, "which I consider very lucky for me." She yanked her water basin from Selwyn's hand, coming close—he was sure—to taking several fingers with it. "I'd consider it luckier still if you ended up dead, too." She turned her back, her hair whipping across his face, and she stamped her feet all the way back into her house. Then she slammed the door, leaving the air vibrating behind her.

Slowly Selwyn turned to face the door of the tavern. He crooked his finger at Farold, half expecting that—if his face showed half of what he felt—Farold would prefer Elswyth's company to his.

But Farold followed him back into the tavern's kitchen.

"'And Farold wasn't even too bad-looking,'" Farold grumbled, as though that were the worst of what Anora had said.

"She called off the betrothal?" Selwyn asked from between clenched teeth, fighting to keep his hands off Farold's little neck. "I kept asking, 'Is there anything you can think of that I should know?' and you didn't think to mention that Anora canceled the betrothal? Are there any other little details you've left out, like

—for example—maybe somebody said, 'Farold, I'm going to kill you'? Maybe you forgot to mention that?" Selwyn realized he was close to shouting, and in his own voice. He took several deep breaths.

"What difference could it make to you, considering your circumstances, that Anora and I had a little falling-out? Besides"—Farold ruffled his feathers—"I didn't think she meant it when she said she wouldn't marry me. I thought she'd get over it."

"What?" Selwyn asked in disbelief.

"She never actually said at the time why she was so angry. Don't forget I didn't know that Kendra—falsely, remember?—accused me of fathering a child. It's not my fault."

"Nothing ever is," Selwyn grumbled. But he was remembering the morning before Farold had been killed, when he'd seen Anora in the market and he'd thought she'd hinted that there was something wrong between her and Farold. *I WASN'T mistaken,* he told himself, even while he remembered that later, at the hearing in Bowden's house, Anora had denied it, leaving him to sound like a fool—or a liar. He also remembered all the weeping she'd done.

"There's probably something else you should know," Farold said.

"Oh?" Selwyn said testily. "What?"

"She was so angry that she was almost incoherent; but one thing I know she said was 'Just wait until I tell my father.'"

Selwyn let that thought settle in. Bowden knew—

or thought he knew—that Farold had disgraced his daughter with Kendra. Another angry father.

But it was hard to think of Bowden when his mind kept going back to Anora. Kind, sweet, gentle Anora. Who, apparently, settled between him and Farold by determining which was the more lucrative match. Who was then willing to switch back when that arrangement failed. Who did a convincing job as the grief-stricken betrothed. Who was willing to call Kendra names and try to beat her with a washbasin. Who at the very least had just ill-wished him, and maybe even threatened him.

He looked down at his hands, at the red welts caused when Anora had snatched the basin away. It seemed Anora was capable of much that he never would have guessed. Slowly he held up fingers seven and eight—two more suspects to add to the list of possible murderers: Anora and her father.

NINETEEN

It had been so long since he had slept in a bed instead of on the hard ground that Selwyn overslept.
Kendra's parents must have decided he needed the rest,
for they didn't wake him.

By the time he got up, it was already light out, and
he could smell bread baking—proof that Wilona, at
least, was already hard at work.

He dressed, fumbling a bit with the unfamiliarity of
women's garb, and arrived in the tavern's common
room just in time to see his father—his real father—
being settled down into his chair in the corner. People
took turns with guard duty, he had learned yesterday,
so that his father was watched even while he was

asleep. Last night had apparently been the turn of Raedan and his brother Merton. They were just leaving, looking bleary-eyed from the long night.

Good, Selwyn thought at them. *Suffer.*

His late start probably worked out for the best anyway, he thought. To talk to his father at Holt's blacksmith shop this morning he would have had to evade the two brothers—eager to be finished and getting home—as well as Holt. Not much chance, probably, to talk privately. It would be easier here. But he had to speak soon, Selwyn knew. From what people said yesterday, today was the last day. No one believed Selwyn could have survived in the cave this long. At sunset his father would be released, and Selwyn needed to talk to him before he did something foolhardy or irrevocable.

"Good morning," Selwyn said to each of Kendra's parents: Orik, checking the volume of ale left in the barrels, and Wilona, kneading dough in the kitchen. "Shall I take some of your delicious bread in to the prisoner?"

Wilona had to stop to think. "Rowe's not a prisoner," she said, though in Selwyn's estimation anyone who was tied to a chair and guarded all day was a prisoner. "And his wife will be bringing him food shortly."

"At least a drink would be a kindness," Selwyn argued, and Wilona shrugged.

Selwyn filled a cup, and brought it in to his father. He intentionally stood between his father and Orik, and placed his back to Orik before he crouched down by the chair. He couldn't tell his father the truth, not all of it, rushed and with the danger of someone walking in on them at any moment. He whispered, very quietly, "I have something to tell you. Try not to react."

Until that moment his father had seemed vague and listless, his eyes almost unfocused as though he was hardly aware of the presence of anyone else in the room. Now those eyes locked on to Selwyn's, piercing but wary, as though by pure force of will he could learn all in a moment whatever it was Selwyn had to say.

Selwyn whispered, "Here, drink some of this." And after his father dutifully obeyed, Selwyn said, "Selwyn is alive and well—don't react." He did not think of his father as a demonstrative man, but he could see the hope and joy in that brief intake of breath, and it was crucial that he didn't attract Orik's attention away from the ale barrels. "Trust me," Selwyn continued, "as long as you just continue as before and don't give them any reason to suspect that you've heard any news, all will be well." Not that he had any way to know that for sure.

"Where is he?" Selwyn's father whispered back.

He couldn't very well answer, *Right here.* "Safe," he said instead. "Truly. Drink some more so Orik doesn't become suspicious."

His father's eyebrows went up at that—Kendra calling her father by his given name—but he took a swallow of ale.

Then, because he was asking his father to take so much on faith, Selwyn added, "There's a back way into the caves, on the far side of the Grandfather Hill. A friend came"—Elswyth would probably smack him for daring to call her a friend—"and showed Selwyn to a safe place." Penryth wasn't safe, but he was simplifying.

"You?" Selwyn's father asked.

It took him a moment to untangle this, to realize his father hadn't seen he was an impostor, despite the mistake about Orik's name. He was simply asking whether he—Kendra—was the friend who had shown Selwyn the way out of the cave.

"No." He didn't dare admit the benefactor was a witch, for he didn't want his father to worry. He did the best he could. "Someone who can help him. They have a plan to reveal the true murderer."

His father closed those terrible hungry eyes for a moment. Then he whispered, "I want to believe..."

Selwyn thought back to the day this had all started, when he and his father had been working to clear the field. He said, "Selwyn told me to tell you that you were right about Anora, and you were right about the big, sturdy girl." The joke had been between them that day, with no one else to overhear.

His father closed his eyes again and breathed deeply.

"I must go," Selwyn said, for every sentence—every moment together—increased the likelihood of his making some blunder that would either reveal the truth or make his father decide Kendra was crazy: each bad in its own way. "Tell Nelda so she doesn't worry." He had been planning to go to Bowden's house himself, but after the things Anora had said last night, he feared that might not be safe.

"Thank you," his father said with such heartfelt warmth that Selwyn had to fight the urge to tell him everything, despite the danger. There would be time for that later. He hoped.

He heard a strange whistling that was not quite bird-like, not quite human, and turned to see Farold sitting on the window ledge.

Without acknowledging him, Selwyn went to the back part of the building, to the living quarters. In a moment Farold appeared at that window.

"What have you learned?" Selwyn asked.

"That it's difficult being a bat in a goldfinch's body. I don't know what goldfinches eat, but I still crave bugs, and I still want to eat all night and sleep all day, but goldfinches' eyes aren't that good for seeing at night, and I can't make that little sound that helped me find my way around when I was a bat, and—"

"Farold!" Selwyn said in exasperation. "You're babbling. I meant, did you find out anything important?"

Farold snorted. "You try catching your supper in the dark, and tell *me* that isn't important."

Selwyn clenched his teeth. "Have you found out anything about the murder?"

Farold sighed—loudly. "Wasn't I just trying to explain to you that it took me all night just to eat enough that I'm not faint with hunger?"

It was Selwyn's turn to sigh. "So, nothing," he said. "What you're saying is that you learned nothing."

Farold opened his beak and cawed like a crow.

"Oh, shut up," Selwyn told him. "All right. Since it's all up to me, what I want to do is visit the room where you were murdered."

"If it's all up to you, why are you bothering to tell me?"

"Farold," Selwyn cried in exasperation.

Suddenly Farold began his best imitation of a goldfinch, which Selwyn guessed was purely to be an annoyance, but a moment later he felt Wilona's hand on his shoulder.

"Poor dear," Kendra's mother said. "I know you feel bad about Farold being killed. But you must accept he *is* dead. Get a grip on reality, dear." Shaking her head, she walked away.

Strange sounds were coming out of Farold's goldfinch beak.

"Are you coming with me," Selwyn asked, "or are you going to stand there laughing?"

"Oh, I'll accompany you," Farold said. "I would hate to miss any of the fun."

TWENTY

After Selwyn finished the morning's chores in the tavern, he told Kendra's parents that the nuns at Saint Hilda's had said fresh air was very important to keep goldfinches healthy—especially caged goldfinches. "The two of us are going out for a walk," Selwyn told them. "We'll be back before the customers come."

If Kendra's parents found this odd, they didn't say so.

As he walked down the street carrying the birdcage, people waved and called greetings. Pretty tavern girls, Selwyn decided, could get away with much that would bring ridicule to farmers' sons.

The mill sat alone on the outskirts of Penryth, since

it needed to be directly on the stream, and the constant noise of the wheel going around day and night was enough to keep people from building their houses too near.

When Selwyn got there, he looked in the doorway and saw the only customer was Snell's widow. Linton was just tying up a sack of flour for her. *Good,* Selwyn thought. Even better than he had hoped. Widow Snell's hands were gnarled and crippled; she'd need Linton's help to get that flour home. Selwyn walked a little bit farther, to where the cultivated fields started—this would be Raedan and Merton's uncle's, the farm closest to the village. When he turned back, the widow and Linton were already far down the street heading in the opposite direction, Linton lugging the bag of flour over his shoulder.

Selwyn returned to the mill, and only old Derian was there.

Hastily, before Derian looked up, Selwyn glanced around the room. Most of the homes in Penryth didn't have locks, for everybody knew everybody; but many of the businesses did—since it was foolish to tempt people beyond what they could withstand. Selwyn saw a heavy board leaning against the wall by the door and knew that at night that board would be placed into the brackets on either side of the door frame. It would take several men and a great deal of noise and splintering of wood to get through that way. No wonder Thorne had said the murderer must have entered through the window. But it didn't have to be Farold's bedroom window, Selwyn thought, even though that one had been open. He would check them all for signs of forced entry, he thought, if there was time. In this room there was only one window, which faced away from the town—toward that field belonging to Raedan and Merton's uncle.

Now, in his Kendra voice, he said, "Hello." He had to say it twice before Derian looked up and smiled at him. Selwyn continued, "This morning I was thinking I needed to take my songbird out for a walk, and also I've been away for so long I thought I just had to see everything and everybody again." *Don't chatter,* Selwyn told himself. *Don't explain too much.*

But Derian didn't comment on what Selwyn had said. He only answered, "Always pleased to have a pretty visitor."

Selwyn felt his face go red, even though Derian was complimenting Kendra, not him. He set the birdcage down on the table, and—as he and Farold had arranged—brushed against the loosely tied binding that held the tiny door closed. "Oh!" Selwyn cried helplessly as the twine fell off and Farold flew out of the cage. "Oh, come back, little bird!" Selwyn felt like a perfect fool, but Derian gallantly jumped to his feet to help.

Farold landed on a stack of flour sacks and waited until Derian was within two steps before taking off again and flying around the room.

Selwyn chased after Farold, but Farold hopped from table to cage top to windowsill.

"Oh, please," Selwyn cried, "close the door and window before he gets out."

Farold flew away from the window but then he went right over Derian's head and out the still-open door. He immediately landed on top of the water barrel by the side of the door.

"Help me!" Selwyn urged Derian, lest the old miller give up.

Derian followed Farold outdoors.

"I'll get the shutters in here," Selwyn called, "in case he comes back in." The shutters, he saw, were fastened by a simple latch. Someone *might* be able to open it from the outside, though Selwyn would have expected scratches on the wood if that were the case, and there weren't any.

Meanwhile, he saw that outside Farold went from the water barrel to a low tree branch. As Derian approached, Farold fluttered to another branch on the other side of the tree, then in a moment flew to sit on top of a nearby bush—all the while enticing Derian to follow by staying almost within reach.

As soon as Derian was out of sight, Selwyn headed for the stairs. The mill was the only building in Penryth that had two stories, to accommodate the huge gears needed to turn the millstone. According to Farold, Derian's room was upstairs, in the front. Farold's was the smaller room in the back beneath the stairs, where he could keep an eye—and ear—on things.

Derian's room first, Selwyn decided, to check that window while he had the most time, for Selwyn could think of no explanation to give if Derian came back and found him there.

Upstairs was the big room that housed the gears and

shafts for the mill wheel. There was only one window, too small for any adult to fit through, and facing—once again—the farm of Raedan and Merton's kinsman. On the opposite wall was a door that opened to overlook the giant waterwheel that turned in the stream. No one could have climbed up and in through there.

In Derian's room the shutters didn't seem to have been tampered with, and, besides, an intruder would have needed a ladder to reach it, for there were no tall trees close enough. Selwyn looked out and saw Derian, almost to the blacksmith shop now, still chasing the goldfinch. But someone else might come in, looking for the miller; or Linton might return. Selwyn needed to hurry.

Back downstairs, he opened the door to Farold's room. Certainly he had known that Farold's body was no longer there: He knew, in fact, better than most, exactly where both Farold and his body were. And there was no reason to expect that after all this time he'd find blood-soaked mattress and blankets. *Somebody* would have taken those away. Considering the circumstances, he didn't know why he was so squeamish to look upon a room where a man had died.

Already, after not quite a week, the room had a dusty, unused smell. The bedding was gone, though Selwyn could tell where it had been, from the space beneath the window. No bloodstains, no evidence that a man's life had ended in violence here. Beyond that was the clothes chest Farold had told him about, where he had kept the knife. Selwyn went through the things in there, feeling unsettled at handling possessions that

Farold would never again use, rummaging through clothes Farold would never again wear—though he had Farold's permission to be here. Clothes, a length of twine, a few coins, an apple gone all soft and brown. In a corner, beneath everything else, was a small stone that seemed to have no purpose except that it sparkled. Had Farold ever been the kind of boy to pick up a stone just because it was pretty? Selwyn realized that after seventeen years of living in the same village with Farold, he didn't know. He closed the chest.

Merton—or someone else, if Merton had bragged about having found the knife—might have looked for the blade in the chest, for it was a logical place to keep such a thing. But Merton had no reason to kill Farold.

So, suppose the murderer *hadn't* known about the knife. Selwyn thought—as he had thought before—a murderer doesn't enter a room and *then* look for something with which to kill his intended victim. Could the murderer have brought a different weapon, dropped it, and only then had to rely on what was at hand? He—or she—might not have even realized that the knife was Selwyn's until the next day.

On the other hand, Selwyn thought, how deep a sleeper was Farold to sleep through someone not only climbing in through his window but also dropping one weapon and searching the room for another?

And if the murderer had dropped or left behind anything, wouldn't it have been found by Linton when he discovered the body, or by Derian after Linton called him in, or by Bowden and Thorne when they examined the room, or by the women who had prepared Farold's body for burial? And if there was such a thing and none of them had found it and it hadn't been cleaned up, or trampled, or covered since, how was Selwyn to even recognize it as being something that didn't belong in the room?

Selwyn turned to the window. Yet another reason— he told himself—why he had been suspected, as if the argument with Farold, and the knife, and the fact that he had been in the vicinity weren't enough: The window was a small one. He was skinny and short and could easily fit through. Holt certainly could not, nor could Bowden, and probably not Orik.

He opened the shutters and found that—beyond the stream that drove the mill wheel—he had a clear view of the back of Bowden's house. He felt what he knew was an unreasonable surge of jealousy: Farold had been able to watch Anora's comings and goings from here.

Not that it makes any difference now, Selwyn thought, what with one thing and another.

The stream would have prevented easy access to the window. *Not likely one of the women then,* Selwyn thought. Not without a lot of determination. He thought about Anora and Wilona, and decided not to dismiss either one of them after all.

He leaned far out the window to look at the narrow stretch of ground between the wall and the water. If there had been footprints, a week's worth of weather had covered them over. He didn't know if anyone had looked that first morning; that was not information they had shared while they were condemning him. There were no muddy footprints on the windowsill or the floor, at least not anymore. The shutters were badly scratched, but most of the scratches looked quite old. Selwyn suspected that Farold may well have sneaked in and out of this window nights when he didn't want his uncle knowing where he was—like the time he had gone to the tavern and spied Alden at the smithy.

Without warning, Farold practically flew into his face. "Move!" Farold cried. "Get out! He gave up and he's coming back."

Selwyn slammed the shutters closed, but they bounced halfway open again. As he reached to grab them a second time, he heard a step in the doorway behind him.

"Well, well," Derian said, "what have we here?"

"I...," Selwyn said, "I thought I saw my bird fly around the side of the mill, and I thought he might come back inside if I opened one of the windows in the back."

Derian leaned forward to hear. "The bird?" he asked.

Selwyn pointed. "He's sitting in that tree across the stream."

Farold had the sense to stay where he was and to chirp a little goldfinch song.

"But you decided to give up," Derian pointed out. "You were just shutting the window."

"He's too full of himself—playing games. Either he'll come back or he won't." *Fool! Fool!* Selwyn called himself. Each thing he said sounded less likely than the last.

Whether he heard the lame explanation or not, Derian said, "You wanted to see Farold's room." No question, just an observation.

There was no use denying it any longer. "Yes," Selwyn admitted.

"I've heard the two of you were friends," Derian said, his voice gentle. "Good friends. Very good friends. I understand why you'd want to see his room, touch his things."

Selwyn inwardly groaned. Were he and Farold the only two in Penryth who hadn't been familiar with that rumor about Farold and Kendra? Still, it couldn't hurt now to have Derian believe this story. It was an excuse for curiosity. Selwyn folded his hands in front of him and looked down at them, not admitting, but neither denying. On the other hand, there was something about the way Derian said "touch" that made Selwyn's skin feel dirty.

Derian apparently took his lack of answer as grief over the dead Farold. "There, there," he said, "what's done is done. Being sad won't bring the boy back."

It wasn't what Selwyn expected from the uncle of the dead man. He looked up, startled. *Surely I'm misjudging things here,* Selwyn told himself, for what he judged was that Derian's smile had less and less gentleness to it, and more and more of a leer.

"Don't be afraid," Derian said, moving closer. "I know you have a kind and gentle heart—didn't I tell you that at the tavern yesterday? We can comfort each other. You, after all, still have your family. I'm all alone now."

It was the same tune he'd been singing yesterday, which didn't make Selwyn like him any better, for he was beginning to suspect Derian was only trying to make Kendra feel sorry for him.

Selwyn took a step back. "No," he said firmly, to make sure Derian heard. If Derian took one more step, that would get him far enough away from the door that Selwyn would have the opportunity to dart past him. The other choice was to knock him down, which Selwyn was reluctant to do. The old man was making offensive suggestions, but—supposing Selwyn to be Kendra—he didn't know just how offensive they were. Still, Selwyn was angry on Kendra's behalf.

"Come, come," Derian said. "I may be old, but I'm wealthy. Yet, what good is wealth, if one is alone? Together we can overcome our sorrow about Farold." Derian took that extra step, and Selwyn dashed past him.

"Come again for another visit," Derian called after him as Selwyn swept up Farold's cage and made for the outside door. "My age is not so terrible to Anora. She has come to like me since Farold died. I have money and energy enough for both of you."

Aghast at what Derian was saying—never mind that the man was old enough to be Kendra's grandfather, never mind that Selwyn wasn't really Kendra—Selwyn hurried out into the street.

Farold landed on Selwyn's shoulder and made a sound of disgust. "Did my uncle just suggest to you what I think he suggested?"

Selwyn glared. Then he tried to force a more pleasant expression onto his face as he noted villagers were looking at him.

"Uh-oh," Farold said. "This looks like trouble heading right toward us."

Selwyn saw that Bowden was approaching, flanked by Thorne and Linton.

And—worst of all—several steps behind were Orik and Wilona. And, with them, carrying a bundle that could only be a baby, was their daughter, Kendra.

TWENTY-ONE

He could, Selwyn supposed, try to convince every-body that he was the real Kendra, and that this newer arrival was an impostor. But he realized—truth be told—he'd been lucky he'd fooled people as long as he had. If it came to answering questions about Kendra's childhood or her family, he'd be revealed as soon as the questions got more complicated than "What are the names of your parents?"

In fact, the real Kendra had probably already an-swered such questions to everybody's satisfaction. She had probably convinced Orik and Wilona before they'd brought the matter to Bowden.

Selwyn dropped the birdcage and started to run in the opposite direction, Farold flying right beside him.

"Stop her!" Linton yelled. "She's a witch, and the bird is her demon familiar!"

Which was probably, Selwyn thought as he ran, just as bad a thing to be accused of as being a murderer. Hands reached out to grasp at him. The long skirt threatened to trip him at every step. Selwyn swerved to avoid a cluster of villagers and dashed between two buildings: Bowden's house and the tavern. Then he made for the stream.

"Wait," Farold shouted.

Selwyn jumped in, just as Farold yelled, "Don't!"

The water momentarily closed over his head. *The dress will weigh me down and be the death of me,* Selwyn thought, but a moment later he found the surface and began swimming. Halfway across the stream he realized something was wrong; with each stroke he was looking at his sleeve, but it was not the sleeve of the dress he had been wearing when he dived in. It was the sleeve of his own shirt: the one he'd been wearing when he'd been imprisoned in the burial cave, the one Elswyth had bespelled, twice.

Selwyn pulled himself up onto the far side. Farold landed on a branch that had gotten washed onshore, and he shouted, "You dumb twit! What did you go and ruin the spell for? Now you'll never be able to convince them you're the real Kendra."

Selwyn saw villagers approaching from both across the stream and on this bank, coming around either side of the mill and leaving him nowhere to run. There was no getting away from them. Still, though they were cutting off escape, they were not closing in. Having seen him change from Kendra to the imprisoned and presumably dead Selwyn in front of their very eyes, no one was willing to be the first to get too close. He sat on the bank, gasping for air, for he was not a strong swimmer, and he told Farold, "I'd never be able to convince them, anyway." He ran his hands down his arms and wrapped his arms around himself—his own self. "How did you know?"

"How did I know what?"

"That immersing myself in water would counteract the spell."

Farold looked skeptical. "You didn't know that? You let her put a spell on you without knowing what the antidote was? You dumb twit, I can't believe you never asked how to get rid of the disguise. *I* asked her. I asked her the first time, when she wasn't even putting a spell on *me*. I assumed you did, too, before you let her actually start. Dumb twit."

It was, eventually, Merton who was the first to actually take hold of his arm, to force him to his feet. "Selwyn," he said hesitantly, incredulously, but clearly into the silence of at least half the villagers, and the rest still gathering. "Is that who you really are: Selwyn?"

Linton had swum across the stream, unwilling to let others take credit for the capture. "Murdering my cousin wasn't enough," Linton shouted so that the people on both sides of the stream could hear. "Obviously Selwyn is deeply involved in sorcery, too! I say we weigh him down with stones and drown him."

"Linton—," Selwyn started, but Linton spun him

around. Merton was still holding on to his arm, so that it was twisted painfully high behind his back. Selwyn gasped in pain, and the next moment, Linton shoved a gag into his mouth. They were not going to let him speak. He had learned things, but they were not going to let him speak.

And then, suddenly, Farold came diving out of the sky, straight at Linton's face.

Startled, Linton threw his arm up to protect his face, letting go of the gag. But in the next moment, Linton recovered enough to swat at the air around his head.

Farold came at him again.

Selwyn spit out the gag. "No!" he cried, knowing that Linton needed only a glancing blow to crush the life out of those delicate bat-disguised-as-bird bones. "Don't!"

And, before he could warn Linton what he was about to do, Linton's hand struck the goldfinch, hurling the bird downward to the ground.

Farold hit with a small but solid thump.

"No," Selwyn said again, this time little more sound than the air being knocked out of his lungs. He jerked free of Merton's hold and threw himself to his knees. But there obviously was nothing to be done. The bird lay perfectly still, its neck twisted, its legs limp, not the slightest stirring of breath. Still, Selwyn picked up the almost weightless body.

Selwyn felt hot, cold, light-headed, and made of stone all at once. After all the bickering and complaining, the disparaging remarks, the times he had thought he'd be so much better off alone than with Farold's help—he gladly would have given up more years to Elswyth in exchange for feeling a heartbeat in the tiny creature's chest.

There was none.

Linton shook his shoulder roughly, jostling his arm, so that the bird's body fell from Selwyn's hand, dropping once more to the grassy ground. "Here, that's enough of that," Linton said gruffly. "No more spells and such."

Selwyn got to his feet. He wanted very much to hurt Linton, and the best way to do this was to tell him exactly what he had done.

But the knowledge was too terrible, and—after all—Linton was only a fool and a bully.

Farold was dead—again—and there was no reason his cousin had to know he had died twice, that Linton himself was responsible for this latest death.

People were murmuring, "What's going on?" and "How can this be?" Some looked dumbfounded, some frightened.

Across the stream, Bowden wore the expression Bowden wore best: furious. "I gave orders," he started, as though in the face of obvious magic, death, lies, and plots, all he could grab hold of was the thought that he had decreed Selwyn was to die, and Selwyn hadn't.

Farold had been dead long before Selwyn had started to get used to him, to begin to like him. *He wasn't that bad. He wasn't as bad as sitting down on a tack.* It wasn't fair, but there wasn't anything that could be done.

Selwyn had to go on alone. "I meant nobody any harm," he said, speaking to everyone, not just Bowden or Linton. "I'm sorry I abused your kindness." *That* was meant particularly for Kendra and her family, who were among those standing on the far bank. "I only wanted time to learn who had really killed Farold."

"*That*," Bowden said, "has already been determined to everyone's satisfaction. And now, besides murder, you are evidently involved in sorcery."

"And what have you learned?" Raedan called out, ignoring Bowden. "Anything?"

Selwyn took a deep breath. The murderer wasn't likely to be Merton, who knew about the knife but had no cause to kill Farold. It couldn't be Bowden or Holt, who couldn't have gotten into the mill. Linton, Anora, Thorne, Orik, and Wilona all had reasons to want Farold dead and could have gone through—or, in Orik's case, squeezed through—Farold's window. But there was only one person he knew of who could easily have learned about the knife without Farold's knowing, who would have had access to Farold's room, and who— from what Selwyn had learned—might well have wanted Farold out of the way. He announced, "I believe it was the miller."

There was a murmur of disbelief from those gathered around.

"You lie." The quavering old voice was Derian's. He stood looking at them from the back window of the mill. Farold's window. "You lie," he repeated. "Why would I?"

Selwyn looked around until he found Anora. "For

the same reason everyone thought *I* wanted Farold dead. To win Anora."

Anora covered her mouth with her hands, which made her expression hard to read.

Derian laughed. "I'm an old man," he said.

Selwyn told the people, "I found that when Derian thought I was Kendra..." He wasn't quite sure how to word this.

The real Kendra put her hand on her hip and tossed her hair. "Derian Miller can't keep his hands to himself," she said. "I'll tell you *that*. He makes all sorts of promises."

"To Kendra?" Anora cried to Derian. "You arranged with my father to marry *me*."

"What?" Derian said, his hearing conveniently fading.

Kendra ignored him. "Oh no," she said to Anora, sounding—Selwyn thought—more sympathetic than condemning. "Surely you didn't believe him?"

Anora grew tight-lipped. "Don't speak to me," she snapped. "At least I know to make the man wait until we're married. *I* didn't try to leave a baby with the nuns of Saint Hilda's."

Kendra hugged her baby closely. She held her head high though her voice shook. "At least I loved the man, not his money."

"*Which* man?" Anora jeered. "Farold, or Derian? They *both* offered to marry me."

"Neither," Kendra said. "And for all that, I think I have fared better than you."

I offered, too, Selwyn thought. *I wanted to marry you,*

once. Did Anora not mention him because his love was not relevant now, or because he had never counted? It made no difference, but it still hurt.

Anora glowered at Kendra. "Slut," she said.

"Enough." Bowden looked from Anora to Kendra to Derian to Selwyn. He said, "None of this is to the point. I will not have my daughter's name and reputation sullied. The arrangement our family made with Derian after Farold died is not of concern to the entire village."

"*Soon* after Farold died," Wilona called out.

Bowden looked ready to knock her down: two parents, protecting their children. "The point is"—he jabbed his finger at Selwyn to emphasize his words—"it was your knife that killed Farold."

"My knife," Selwyn said, "that I lost, that Merton found, and that Merton gave to Farold." He turned on Merton, who looked as though he would deny it.

But after a moment's hesitation, Merton nodded, saying, "This is true."

"Oh, I'm sure it is," Bowden snorted. "But why tell it only now?"

"I was afraid," Merton said, "that if people knew Farold had the knife..."—he looked helplessly at Selwyn and finished all in a rush—"they would consider that one more reason for Selwyn to hate Farold and want him dead: to get the knife back."

Suddenly Merton's silence made sense. Selwyn could see people looking at him suspiciously even now. *Just when I needed you, Farold,* he thought, but it wasn't anger or annoyance he felt. He said to Merton, "Except how would I know Farold had it unless you told me, or Farold did, before he died? Obviously Farold had no call to tell me..."

"Nor did I," Merton told the people.

The villagers glanced at each other as though to see if anybody could tell what Selwyn was trying to say.

They had already seen him change form before their very eyes. He told the rest of it. "I sought help from a witch," he said, "the same witch who changed my appearance. Through her, I learned the truth from Farold after he was dead."

"What nonsense—," Bowden started.

"Or rather, I learned from his spirit." And still Selwyn held some back for Linton's sake, not to say, "He was alive and well, and you rashly killed him," unwilling to force the man to live with that knowledge. *Farold, why did you have to get in the way?* Selwyn had to take another deep breath to keep from shaking.

"Lies," Derian said.

"Pathetic lies," Bowden amended.

"Farold told me he kept the knife in his room," Selwyn said, "and there Derian could easily get to it."

"Farold's room was his own," Derian said. "I didn't go in there."

"You're in there now."

Derian threw his arms up in exasperation. "Because *you* were in here," he protested. "You—disguised as Kendra—opened the shutters."

"Enough of this," Bowden told Linton. "Gag him and bring him back to my house until we decide what's to be done with him."

"You *did* go in there," Selwyn said to Derian as Linton bent to pick up the rag. He spoke in a rush. "In front of Holt Blacksmith yesterday you admitted you'd seen me the night of the murder. You described me, trying to get Anora to come to the window." He found Holt in the crowd, and Holt was nodding.

"I remember," Holt told everyone.

Linton hesitated.

Selwyn finished, "But your room is in the front of the mill, Derian, overlooking the street."

Derian licked his lips. "I couldn't sleep that night. I...thought I heard a noise in Farold's room, so I went to look. The shutters were open—that was what I heard, one of them rattling—and I looked out the window and saw you. You must have come in through there after I went back to bed."

Thorne said, "You heard the shutters rattling when you normally can't hear a customer banging on your front door? When you told us you slept soundly all night? When you told us you didn't hear a thing?"

"I meant after that," Derian said lamely. "Farold was my boy. You can't imagine I'd kill him. Don't you remember when his father was the miller, and the mill caught fire? I rushed into the flames and rescued him. I raised him as a son."

Selwyn remembered when he and Farold had been talking to Elswyth about Thorne's son, Alden, burning down the smithy, and Elswyth had said, "Just because a fire starts during a storm doesn't mean the storm caused the fire." Now, he said, "Farold was fortunate you were close by that night. And you, of course, were fortunate that only the living quarters burned—only people died—and the machinery wasn't damaged. I remember everyone patting you on the back, calling you a hero. But I say you were there to make sure the mill itself didn't go up in flames; I say you rescued Farold only so people wouldn't wonder why you were there. No one asks what a hero is doing so close to the disaster. It's obvious: rescuing poor little orphan nephews."

"Lies," Derian repeated. But this time Bowden didn't agree with him.

Selwyn said, "You've been in the habit of killing to get what you want for a dozen years now."

"Boy, this witch of yours has affected your mind," Derian said.

Which everyone knew was no answer.

Derian disappeared from the window.

"Murderer!" Linton shouted, pushing past Selwyn, not even seeing him. "You murdered your own kins-people."

It was over. With that, Selwyn knew it was over.

Other people began shouting, running. Someone screamed to stop the miller—that he would try to set fire to the mill, to take everything with him.

Oh, Farold, Selwyn thought, looking down at the insignificant little bird's body in the grass. From the beginning, he had known it would have to come down to this. For everyone—eventually, one way or anoth-er—everything came down to this. *But not in such a way,* Selwyn thought.

He could hear the thumping of feet in the mill

building, downstairs, upstairs, and then the shutters on the side slammed open, those on the second floor that overlooked the giant waterwheel. By the sounds, Derian flung himself out. By the sounds, he must have hit the wheel. Several times. People gasped or screamed, and moved in closer, but still Selwyn couldn't look up to see what was happening, couldn't look away from what had already happened.

Eventually, he walked back to the tavern, to find his father and his mother.

TWENTY-TWO

According to the bargain Selwyn had made with Elswyth, he had four days left to spend with his family before his nine and a half years of servitude began.

His mother wept and urged flight, pointing out that if there were enough miles between Selwyn and the witch, the spell to summon him might not work. If they could get on a boat, she was sure that the sea separating them would diminish the strength of the tug of magic.

His father said to let the spell call Selwyn. He would go, too, and chop off the witch's head.

"Father," Selwyn said, "no. I agreed. She fulfilled her part of the bargain. I will do this."

"We'll see," his father said in that tone that meant his mind was perfectly well made up already.

And so, to avoid certain disaster, Selwyn left home after only three days.

He told his parents—which was true—that he was going into the village to say good-bye to Kendra. He just did not tell them that he would not return to say good-bye to them.

He had already walked beyond the fields, beyond even the path that led up into the hills. He had walked to where the road curved and dipped right before the start of the woods when, around the curve, came a tall young woman—a goose girl, apparently, for a large ungainly white duck waddled along beside her.

The duck lifted its wings, but they must have been clipped, for it stayed earthbound. The creature charged toward Selwyn, its wings extended and flapping, looking as awkward as a young child running soon after learning to walk.

Selwyn braced himself, though ducks are not generally so aggressive as geese.

The duck wrapped its wings around Selwyn's leg and said, "Selwyn, you dumb twit, I'm amazed but happy that you're still alive! What happened, did you get confused, you're coming a day too early, how did you escape?"

"Farold?" Selwyn said.

"How many talking ducks do you know?" the duck asked.

Selwyn knelt to sweep him up into his arms. "I didn't know I knew any!" he cried. "And I'm amazed and delighted to see that you're still alive." Which he was —more than he would ever have guessed. "What happened?" he asked. By then the young woman had reached them, and he added, "And who's this?"

The young woman smacked him on the side of the head.

"Oh," he said over the ringing in his ear. "Elswyth." He remembered she had kept saying she was gathering the ingredients for an important spell. Now he saw what the spell must have been. She was young, looking hardly older than he himself. "I would have come," he told her. Turning his attention to Farold, he asked, "And why are you a duck?"

Farold said, "After that dunderhead of a cousin of mine started swatting, I suddenly found myself in the afterlife again—which, I suppose, means he hit me."

Selwyn nodded.

"So, I thought, 'Well, it's one thing for me to be dead, having been through it already and all; it's another thing for the dumb twit to be on his own.' I was certain those villagers were going to toss you into that stream or tear you apart. So I said to myself, 'Well, I can't do anything here, not having a working body anymore, so I'll go get the old witch and see what she can do.'"

Elswyth showed her teeth in a grin.

"Except she's not old anymore," Selwyn observed.

"She was still easy to find. Certain things are easier in the afterlife, you know—even though I can't tell you about it. Not having a body, I haunted her until she got tired of that and gave me one." Farold held his wings up. "Unfortunately, she didn't have too much to choose from. What about you? Did you find out who killed me? The first time, I mean, not counting Linton?"

"Oh," Selwyn said, reluctant to break the news. "I'm afraid it was Derian."

"*Derian?*" Farold said. "My own uncle?"

"I'm afraid so."

Elswyth made a disappointed sound and shook her head. "I was sure it was the beautiful girlfriend," she said.

Farold ignored her. "But you said it wasn't him, because I was running the mill so well."

"*You* said it wasn't him, because you were running the mill so well," Selwyn corrected. "And it had nothing to do with that. It turns out he killed you to win Anora."

"Ha!" Elswyth gave an I-told-you-so smirk.

"It also turns out," Selwyn finished, "that he set the fire that killed your family when you were a child, to get the mill from your father. Everybody turned against him, and he jumped from the upper window and killed himself."

Farold sat down in the dust of the road with a sigh, which sounded odd coming from a beak.

"I'm sorry," Selwyn said.

"It's just quite a shock," Farold told him.

Elswyth sighed also, to indicate she was getting bored.

After a few moments Farold said to Selwyn, "But they let you go, even knowing that witchcraft had been involved in your disguise?"

"I think," Selwyn said, "only because they felt so bad about putting me in the burial cave. But for the most part they wouldn't talk to me, wouldn't look at me if they came face-to-face with me in the street. Anora spit at me, but I think that's because nobody will talk to her, either. It came out that she was going to marry Derian, and everybody saw it was because of the money, and also she said some horrid things to Kendra. And as for Kendra, it turns out the father of her baby is Alden Thorneson."

"Kendra," Elswyth said. "The other beautiful girl with the..." She gestured.

"Poor Kendra," Farold said. "She would have done better with me after all."

Selwyn said, "She was trying to protect Alden, thinking he'd marry her when they were both in Saint Hilda's, but he wouldn't. But Raedan wants to marry her. Apparently he's loved her for years. He wants her and the baby. Kendra and Raedan are some of the only people willing to speak to me—and Kendra, of all of them, has the greatest cause to complain of me."

"Is that why you were leaving early," Elswyth asked, "instead of waiting for the spell?"

"No," Selwyn admitted. "I was afraid my parents might...do something to try to help me."

"Ah," she said.

"It was kind of you to help Farold," Selwyn said, "and to come to see if I needed help." He thought about what he had just said. "Do I owe you more years for that?"

Elswyth gave a tight grin. "At the rate you're going," she said, "you're going to owe me so many years, I'm going to have to cast a spell to make *you* younger, just so that you can serve them all. Three years for the duck, two for walking all this distance, and one more because I warned the duck if he didn't stop quacking, I was going to make you pay one more year."

Fifteen and a half years. Selwyn sighed. "We might as well start now," he said. "Get a day's head start."

Farold said, "*I* was thinking—"

"For a change," Elswyth interrupted.

Farold quacked at her. "*I* was thinking," he repeated to Selwyn, "that what you need is a substitute."

"A substitute *what?*" Elswyth asked testily.

"A substitute to take your place serving the old witch. I volunteer."

"I do not," Elswyth said, "intend to spend fifteen and a half years with you."

"Too bad," Farold said. "Quack, quack, quack, quack, quack."

"Stop it," Elswyth warned icily. "I don't need a spell to stuff you and baste you with cherry sauce."

"I'll haunt you again."

Elswyth folded her arms across her chest. She looked at Selwyn. "You promised," she reminded him in a calm, even voice.

"I did," he agreed. He looked at Farold. "I did," he told him.

"Good," Elswyth said.

Farold's tail feathers drooped.

Elswyth said, "That settled, I release you from your promise."

"What?" Selwyn asked.

"Fifteen and a half years spent in the company of

someone who doesn't want to be there? That would be as bad as fifteen and a half years with the duck. Consider it my birthday present to myself: freedom from your company. Good-bye, Selwyn. Good-bye, duck."

"Wait," Selwyn called as she started back down the road.

Elswyth turned back.

Even young, she was not as beautiful as Anora. She was not lively and fun-loving like Kendra. But she had helped him when nobody else was there. Time and again she had helped him. And she had come to Penryth maybe, he liked to think, because she had thought he was in need of more help. At what point had she stopped expecting that she would ever be repaid?

"A year," Selwyn said, "certainly seems fair. I couldn't very well begrudge a year after all you've done for me."

She looked at him appraisingly.

"*If,*" he added, "you promise to stop hitting. *That* isn't very nice."

"Well," she started out huffily, but then, reluctantly, she forced herself to nod. She said, "I can only try."

And Selwyn could only hope she would try hard.

She gestured for him to join her.

"First," Selwyn said, "we have to go back and explain to my parents, so they don't worry."

"Of course," she said. "Why am I not surprised?"

So they headed, side by side, back to Penryth, with Farold waddling along behind, grumbling, "Isn't there a pond along here somewhere? Ducks need water, you know. All this walking isn't good for webbed feet. You should have brought a basket to carry me in. We'll have to get one in Penryth."

"Don't you have an afterlife to go to?" Elswyth asked.

"Oh," Farold said, "eventually."

DATE DUE

DEC 17 '01	
OCT 21 '03	MAR 02 '07
NOV 4 '03	
FEB 13 '04	
MAR 16 2005	MAY 14 '07
JAN 20 2006	JAN 09 '09
OCT 30 '06 OCT 03 '06	
OCT 30 '06	
JAN 26 '07	

DISCARD